Our Marriage Counselor

Carl Tiktin

THE PERMANENT PRESS
Sag Harbor, NY 11963

For information, address:
  The Permanent Press
  4170 Noyac Road
  Sag Harbor, NY 11963
  www.thepermanentpress.com

Library of Congress Cataloging-in-Publication Data

Tiktin, Carl, author.
  Our marriage counselor / Carl Tiktin.
  Sag Harbor, NY : The Permanent Press, [2017]
  ISBN 978-1-57962-492-7
    1. Humorous fiction.

PS3570.I34 O97 2017
813'.54—dc23   2016044267

Printed in the United States of America

First, to my very lovely and very supportive wife, Colette. She makes it all worthwhile.

Then to my wonderful children—Ross, Michelle, Hope, Laura, and Jacques-Laurent.

Now here come all my grandchildren—Nicole, Michael, Alex, Brett, Eric, and the latest, Benoît.

I'm not through yet—I have great grandchildren: two lovely twin girls, Sienna and Ava.

Chapter One

I would draw me a damn Jew marriage counselor—little soft-living, young Jewboy, kind of sickening sweet smile—his version of the *Today* show who the fuck knows?! Lookit this motherfucka! Maybe his first case. We his damn guinea pigs. What the hell a damn Jew know about problems in a black marriage? Would he try to fix up an Eskimo marriage? Would he get it if the damn wife complained that her old Iki didn't put the blubber on the right slab of ice after he came in from the seal hunt? Shit no!

If this damn woman didn't spend all my bread, wouldn't need a marriage counselor to begin with, would I? Other than pissing away everything I got, she one of the moodiest, dissatisfied women in Queens County. Holds the record for the world's longest bad mood. But now worse of worse she run up all those bills and the credit card company out after my ass. Now what the fuck this motherfucka goin' to do about that!? Pay my bills?!

"Thank you very much for being available for us, Dr. Meltzer," Thaddeus says.

There's a snicker at his side from Beverly.

Thaddeus knew she would do that. She always does that shit to embarrass me, to undermine me, to make me look fucking bad! Bitch!

Beverly hates that he's such a hypocrite. Even though he's such a bigot she knew he was going to start kissing this man's ass the moment they walked in the door. He talks to an educated white man like this one and he tries to sound like a graduate of an Ivy League college. He talks to Joe Sixpack and tries to be "one of the guys." He talks to a black man and he's all motherfucka and high five. He talks to a conservative and he's Clarence Thomas. He talks to a liberal and he's Thurgood Marshall. He talks to a Jew and he's pro-Israel. He talks to a Catholic and he can't praise the Pope enough. He talks to a Democrat and Clinton was great. He talks to a Republican and Reagan was the greatest president who ever lived.

Where is the real Thaddeus Carmichael?

And if she ever finds him, will she even want him?

Thaddeus knows why she snickered. She doesn't get it. When you're a salesman you got to be what the client wants you to be. If he zig you zig and if he zag you zag. Yeah, I know I ain't selling this motherfucka but I got me into the habit and what's wrong with that?! You never know who you going to sell next. Financial Planner of the month last month out of the whole Hillside General Office of the great motherfucking Meridian Life Insurance Company! Eat shit, bitch!! You don't mind spending and overspending a salesman's hard-earned commission but you bitch because of a salesman's ways. That's the way it is in this world—you got to be what the motherfucka wants you to be.

"I'm not a doctor yet," Jonathan Meltzer explains with what he feels is appropriate modesty. "I'm just completing my doctorate this year. You're a little premature."

Premature. Careful, Jonathan thinks, I might be using words these people don't understand.

Thaddeus notices Jewboy's eyes cloud over a bit as he sneaks a look at his own personal bankruptcy machine, Bitch Beverly, née Beverly Thornton Ovington. Jamaican Brit shit. More damn tons in that name than an elephant. I never should have changed it for her. In spite of all her shit though she foxy all right. I like walking down the street with her, especially when I see white boys salivate, thinking where did this nigger deserve something like that. I look like every white man's bad dream of a pushy nigger. Ultra dark skin, spiky whiskers, and big teeth. I look like the big bad fucking bogeyman, don't I Premature Doctor Mister Jonathan Meltzer! Bet you can't figure out how I commandeered a foxy, light-skinned lady like this, can you? Eat shit, motherfucka. You there jerkin' your dick over Angelina Jolie, wind up fucking some bitch with a fat ass and a nose like Barbra Streisand. Best you can get, right?! I'm a goddamn black motherfucka and proud of it! Hear?! Proud of my African heritage. Some-times though, when the shit hittin' the fan like now, I wish I was back there swinging from the trees having a ball. Seen this documentary on the apes on TV—Beverly pissed at me watching anything to do with Africa. This one old boy gorilla goes up behind this one old girl and he gives her a real quick kind of casual butt fuck and then he just strolls away—maybe never sees that bitch again—certainly don't drop no credit cards in her paw. Shit!

Jonathan Meltzer has problems in his new position as counselor in the Jamaica Family Center. He can't get used to the blacks, as he inadvertently thinks of them, and then makes himself think African Americans. He's not been brought up in any way more bigoted than any other Jewish boy from

Merrick, Long Island. His father's a CPA and his mother has a boutique where she sells many as high-fashion dresses as one could hope to sell in Valley Stream, Long Island, and still make a living. The only meaningful association the family has with African Americans is the *schvatza* who comes twice a week to clean the house—a nice, big fat lady who takes the bus from Freeport, smells a little and never really cleans under the furniture . . . but listen what do you expect . . . at least she's honest . . . not that I leave anything around for her to be dishonest about . . . you know what I mean.

There's no one in his house—his parents, his older brother, and younger sister; he's the middle one—who says or does anything other than any other Jewish family says or does about them. They all saw *A Raisin in the Sun* on TV and sympathized with the protagonists, yet they would get nervous if a black family wanted to move in to the neighborhood. Sidney Poitier on the screen is moving and charismatic, but next door he would be threatening and property devaluing. Bigotry is awful but there's no reason for some of them to get so excited about it. Jonathan's a liberal but he hates noise and fuss. Things ought to be done quietly, easily, and naturally. This Sharpton gets a little ridiculous at times. Hey, his grandparents and their generation didn't go through all that. They simply worked hard, sent their kids to good schools, and then quietly took over. That's the right way. But of course he knows when he begins thinking that way he's falling into a nonliberal—almost bigoted—frame of mind so he stops all such thoughts from becoming pervasive.

He's never known or been around any blacks before in the way you get used to people—their rhythm, way of talking, their humor, slang, gait, way of dressing—almost everything. As a result they make him nervous—more so because he doesn't want them to sense that his slight disorientation is caused by prejudice or bigotry or anything like that.

This encounter is even more stressful than usual. Jonathan is attempting to keep his equilibrium, to maintain his cool, to keep in focus, because this woman over on his left, seated next to the black guy, is the woman of every wet dream he's had since he saw Beyoncé in *Dream Girls*. Beverly's light-skinned and curvaceous; her entire look—exotic, deeply sensual, earth-moving. Are those eyes really green-hazel? Are eyes like that possible? Had she looked at him in a pleasurable manner? He never feels very virile and manly. He's tried to take up sports. At first racquetball, but his mother put a stop to it because she felt it was too dangerous, so next tennis but no matter how many lessons he takes he just can't get the hang of the game.

He's twenty-eight years old and wants to get out of the house already and maybe get married if he could find a girl with a decent income to support him until he gets started on his own practice and makes some good money rather than this pittance as an overworked, underpaid social worker-marriage counselor at this community center here on Jamaica Avenue. Actually he's going with a girl now who's a possibility. His therapist hasn't come out with the final word on her yet.

"Now could you give me some idea of why you feel the need for marriage counseling?" Jonathan asks, leaning back on his swivel chair and putting his hands behind his head.

Thaddeus scratches his spiky whiskers. Bad body language, Jewboy. We learn all that body language shit in selling. I used to do that until I went out in the field with my sales manager and got it pointed out to me. That position shows you are uninvolved and detached. It's like you leaning back for a blow job. You're asking the other person you are in contact with to make you take your hands off the back of your head and lean forward and get into it because something here makes you tense. I should tell this motherfucka about that. Give him a little lesson. But why? Shit I ain't here to help him, he's supposed to be here to help me.

Thaddeus waits for Beverly to start because this shit's all her idea to begin with. She'd been trying to get him to a marriage counselor for ages and finally when the credit card shit came up, she said, "Look at the problems we have. I acted out because I wasn't able to talk out the rage I feel when you abuse me the way you do! We have to communicate or our relationship will deteriorate completely and poor Janelle will grow up in a broken home. We need marriage counseling."

"You talkin' like a goddamn Jew!" He bit right back at her. "Marriage counseling and therapy and all that crap is one block of the white man's neighborhood I got no desire to move in to. All them goddamn Jews in my office. Sy Silverstein, Gil Monick, Joe Kahn, they all in fucking therapy. Go around the office saying deep, analytical shit to each other like what you just said—acting out, hostility, get in touch with your feelings, passive, aggressive, appropriate, inappropriate, being taken care of, hang-up. No matter how much therapy these boys get, no matter how many thousands of dollars they cost the company in insurance claims, they still hang on to their witchy Jewish wives while they lurch after one girl, always non-Jewish, or the other. Therapy is a Jewish thing invented by a Jew for Jews so's Jews could have something to hang on to cause their religion don't mean shit to them anymore. Now their spiritual bond has to do with their school of therapy. Do you worship at Temple Freud or Synagogue Eclectic? They talk about the most intimate things, all out in the open. Shit I pass by a bunch of those guys talking loud in the hall or an open office and I hear about small penises, dry pussies, toilet training, incestuous urges toward their own daughters . . . ain't no barriers they respect. It their Chosen

People thing. They're proud to go to the shrinks! Proud to be fucked-up! Normal people would be rightfully ashamed. Their automatic superior attitude is that everyone's fucked-up but only the Jews acknowledge it and actively seek to do something about it. They openly compete on how fucked-up they are. My mother's crazier than yours, my father more passive, my wife more frigid, my shrink more perceptive. If they ever find out my black ass went to a shrink they'd feel threatened and intruded upon, like a black family moving in to a white neighborhood, a white Jewish neighborhood. If a lot of blacks went into therapy they'd sell out in a panic, move out of that neighborhood, and maybe go into Indian spirituality suburbia or something."

"You finished? Let me tell you something, Mr. Thaddeus Carmichael. We are going to marriage counseling or I am taking little Janelle out of this house, moving in with my mother, and then maybe going back to raise my child in Jamaica."

"Ain't no goddamn Jew shrinks in Jamaica!"

"Don't need any there!"

"If that is such an island paradise, why are you here?!"

"My parents brought me here at fourteen. I can go back and work for any of the resorts and make more than enough to raise my child in peace and harmony on a beautiful island with no damn drug dealers outside my door."

Beverly has a degree in hotel management. In Jamaica she would get a high-paying job at any of the resorts and she knows it. So does Thaddeus. Part of him thinks it would be great to get rid of her. Another part doesn't. If she goes, she takes Janelle with her and he couldn't stand that. He tried to stall about going to a marriage counselor but Beverly started to pack, called her mother and told her she's moving back in with the baby. Her mother couldn't wait—she'll clear her old room for her. Beverly's father wanted to come over and cane Thaddeus. Her brother wanted to help. Shit, he didn't do anything wrong. She did. She drove him into debt! But he had to consent to the marriage counseling or she'd leave and he wasn't ready for that. Yet he really feels as if he's betraying an ethic. Used to be when a black couple fought the man just took off, but now with all these mortgages and debts and shit supposed to hang in there and take it at least till the kid is grown like the damn guilt-ridden Jews do. Seems all this equal opportunity bullshit just gives him the same opportunity as the white boy to be a long-suffering fool. Damn how did he get caught up in this shit!

Beverly's impressed with anything Jewish. She puts plastic covers on the furniture, been cooking baked ziti, and makes them go to a damn Chink restaurant in Forest Hills every Sunday—only black family there making all the Jews uncomfortable. Chinks get pissed cause they're afraid they'll lose business and so they get bad service . . . long waits, cold food, no water, stale noodles. When Janelle starts to cry they're afraid the Chinks going to come after them with a meat cleaver they look so pissed. Jews huddle in with each other and whisper about the *schvatza*. Thaddeus wants to crawl into his wonton. Beverly sits there like a proud hen daring anyone to say anything to her. Thaddeus can barely digest his Moo Goo Gai Pan.

Now she just sits there prim and proper kind of blinking her eyes and looking off as if she hasn't the faintest idea what she, Miss Marvelous Bitch Beverly, is doing in such a tacky place with all these niggers and their family problems.

"Well, you see Doctor . . . I'm sorry, Mr. Meltzer," Thaddeus says. "We were going along just fine until I got a call from Visa telling me unless I started to pay off the balance on my credit card they would get in touch with my employer and start an action to garnish my commissions."

"You weren't aware your credit card was overdrawn?"

"No, you see my wife over here . . ." Yeah that woman pretending she's not even here . . . like she's been dropped in from another planet or something . . . studying her nails and brushing some lint off that dress that somehow crept too high up her leg and what the fuck does she think she's doing anyway showing Jewboy all that motherfucking thigh? ". . . was supposed to be taking care of all that. I give her a certain amount of money every week—a generous amount . . . and she pays the bills. I'm too busy to be bothered with minutiae like that."

Bitch don't like that. Feels it's a put-down. Her a mere bill payer. Good. Come on, bitch. Join in the fight.

"I am a busy, productive, financial security consultant," Thaddeus continues. "I work hard. I sell. My whole life is selling. I'm out there in the field hustling all the time. I can't be bothered with paperwork. Hate it! I have a full-time secretary in my office and she does it all but I didn't want my secretary messing with my private bills so I give all that to my wife."

"I'm not complaining about paying the bills," Beverly at last chimes in with the charming lilt she uses when she wants to impress that she comes from the islands and is not a black American.

Thaddeus picks it up. Doesn't that say it all? Uppity. Always was and always will be. Brought up to think her shit don't stink, pisses perfume and shits Mello rolls, his father said about her the first time he saw her but Thaddeus didn't listen because she was all that foxy. Bitch thinks she married beneath her when she married an American black that descended from slaves while she descended from people oppressed by colonizers. Jamaicans swear they adore the British cause they ignore all the centuries of shit pulled on them and concentrate on their shallow mannerisms and their school system and shit.

"Well what about that, Mrs. Carmichael?" Jonathan asks.

She leans forward and fixes Jonathan Meltzer with her beautiful eyes. Intense. Sincere. Limpid green-hazel pools of sensuality. Jonathan's heart goes thrum. She senses it and likes it. Beverly now, once again, suddenly digs white guys. Especially white Jewish guys. And this one has blue eyes—like Sheldon, her last boyfriend before she was stupid enough to get caught with this damn insurance peddler. Sheldon Goldblatt. His father owns a jewelry store on Canal Street. That says it all, girl. The family lives in a condo overlooking the Throgs Neck Bridge. Sheldon would point to their terraced apartment when he drove with her across the bridge in his beat-up Audi. Sheldon could get away with seeing a black girl as long as he was a grungy-looking rock drummer. It was just part of a whole pattern of rebellion—the no-shave no-shower look, the music, the drugs. But then after he went to the hospital because he went berserk on crack, his parents put pressure on him to give up his going nowhere life and come into the jewelry business—take it over so poppa and momma could retire to Florida. Part of the package, get rid of the *schvatza* girlfriend—who they'd met and thought was very pretty but still . . . So Sheldon gave her a long speech. He was going to straighten up, buy a couple of suits, and go into the business. No drugs, no drums, no Beverly. He loved her but could never marry her. No future for her with him. His parents, not him, too bigoted. Then she didn't want to look at another white guy the rest of her life so next thing she knows she's in bed with one of the darkest guys ever placed on this earth—a black hole in more ways than one—and then she's in trouble with this bogeyman as the poppa and that's what put her in the jam she finds herself in today. Caught with a kid, living in a small house in Saint Albans, with an insurance peddler in the house and drug dealers on every corner. A fine rose amongst riff-raff. Now, after two years of marriage, seeing Jonathan, she has a revival of her interest in white guys, white Jewish guys with blue eyes in particular. Jewish guys are sweeter and more pliable than other white guys—the Italians with their muscles and the Irish with their booze. And they all have money in the family. You have to look beyond what they're actually doing at the moment. They can be tending bar in a grimy joint or waiting to be the next Tom Cruise or driving a taxi while writing their great novel or whatever but their fathers are all doctors or lawyers or big businessmen with trust funds waiting for them when they come to their senses—give up all that artist nonsense and come into the family business. But it's too late for Sheldon—he got married to a Barbara and sure enough moved to Roslyn Heights. That fucking bitch leading the life ought to have been hers by right. She should be living and laughing on the north shore of Long Island and then in a few years a mansion on Sands Point.

She fantasizes herself married to someone like this nice little young Jewish boy who would never bother her about anything and be as easy to control as a kitchen blender, living in a big house with her Aunt Evelyn helping with all the kids. She'd give this nice little boy a couple of beautiful kids and he'd give her a carefree life. And maybe, just maybe, one or two of the kids would have blue eyes.

Few people understand what blue eyes mean to an island woman. You don't know what blue is until you see the blue of an island sky. In the islands most eyes are brown or green or hazel but hardly ever blue. Blue eyes mean there's white in your strain—and no matter what anyone says, that puts you ahead of the game. If you have blue eyes the gods have blessed you. She used to dream about giving Sheldon blue-eyed babies and, in her tears, when they were breaking up she told him her dream but he was like a wealthy man sitting in his pot of gold because to him blue eyes meant nothing—his sister had blue eyes and his mother, so what was the big deal?

"I don't believe it will be productive to concentrate on the fact that I might have spent a little more money than I should have spent," she says, enjoying her own educated-by-the-British-System command of the language. "He simply wants to get me on the defense before I have a chance to lay out what he's really like."

"What am I really like?" Thaddeus asks.

"Arrogant, not helpful with the child, expects me to be his housemaid."

"Arrogant?!"

"Before we get into specific issues let me give you an idea of how this ought to work," Jonathan says. Part one—setting parameters before getting in to specific issues. It's vital to go by the book, at least at first, until he becomes adept at how this marriage counseling business is supposed to work. During practice sessions in school they demonstrated the disaster of what could happen if the clients took control of the proceeding.

"We will attempt, at this meeting, to simply define problems—locate them, if you will, like a doctor probing with all the tools in his possession. We will not try to solve anything, make suggestions—nothing like that, though surprisingly, when you start to clearly define problems, solutions immediately come to mind. We will then meet individually. I'll get a chance to know both of you better and you'll get a chance to air some things that might be too difficult to air in front of each other. Then we will meet together again—regroup so to speak—and at that point we will be dealing with solutions to problems that have clearly been brought to the fore. We'll alternate between individual sessions and family group sessions in accordance with how things are going."

He stops and waits for questions.

Canned, Thaddeus thinks. He knows one when he hears one because when he started out in the insurance business they made him memorize a canned sales talk so good he could say it in his sleep, "I imagine, like most of us, Mr. Prospect (substitute actual name of the person you are speaking to) you've had some difficulty in saving and accumulating money through the years, is that so? Well, if I could show you a plan, the finest and most up-to-date plan for saving and accumulating money that has ever been devised, how much do you feel you might be able to put aside, say every week?" Yeah, this motherfucka is brand new at this shit. We like cadavers medical students work on. They wouldn't put no raw motherfucka like this over on Park Avenue, would they? I gotta watch this motherfucka. He don't know shit.

"Now we've got one situation that has emerged." Jonathan turns to Beverly. "Your husband feels you've spent too much." Then to Thaddeus. "And your wife has characterized your attitude as arrogant. Now arrogant is not a concrete term. And we will try to avoid that kind of thing here. One person's version of arrogance might well be another's version of . . . say integrity. It will be important to simply deal with concrete issues without hurtful labels. If you could, Mrs. Carmichael, by the way, I would like very much for us to be on a first-name basis from here on. I'm Jonathan. May I call you . . . ?"

"Beverly," she says breathlessly. Jonathan gets out of her eyes before he starts to melt. God what a woman! He hopes she understands his criticism of the word arrogant is simply a device to put a bar of objectivity between them. He worries about the times when he will have one-on-one sessions with Beverly. Scary yet provocative. He will have to ponder this dilemma. But he's really afraid his pondering might work itself into masturbation. He has an erection now—it's insidious and disturbing. He's had to change his posture, lean forward in case someone suddenly decides to dash behind the desk and spots it protruding shamefully. That, by itself, is no real indication of any kind of problem because he goes around with an erection about 90 percent of his waking hours and about 100 percent of his sleeping hours. He has innumerable wet dreams, remembers them, then masturbates on the experiences he's had in the wet dreams. His therapist, Dr. Timothy Mitchell, has always thought this an unusual phenomenon and has taken notes, with Jonathan's permission, in order to write an article in *Psychology Today*, not identifying Jonathan of course.

Jonathan is almost fever-pitch excited because no matter where he looks there is Beverly Carmichael's thigh, smooth, light brown. The Stones—Brown Sugar how come you taste so good—background music in his brain now. A short lascivious road up her thigh, little black panty—sure it's black lace and then . . . There was one brief shot in *Carmen Jones* of Dorothy Dandridge in a leopard bra and panty and he's never gotten that out of his libido, not that he really tried. The image is old reliable, something he can use to jerk off on in a pinch—when he wants to come fast because his mother is prowling around his bedroom or the cat is at the door—he always feels the cat will see him and tell his mother.

Jonathan turns to Thaddeus. "Thaddeus." Thaddeus announces his name flatly.

"Now I don't know why the man insists on being called Thaddeus. Why not Teddy or Ted?" Beverly suddenly complains.

She's got a point, Jonathan thinks, Thaddeus is so pretentious.

"See there?" Thaddeus retorts. "Does a man have a right to be called as he wants or not? I'm proud of Thaddeus but I think someone who's called Teddy sounds like a damn dog or something. And you know what Ted means?"

"Laid out to dry," Jonathan retorts proudly.

Man do crossword puzzles. "To me, someone calls me Ted is like fighting words. She knows that."

"Now don't you think that Thaddeus is a bit much," Beverly asks, leaning forward. God is that just a bit of cleavage?

"Well, we won't get into right or wrong at this stage. You see I'm not going to be an arbitrator . . . a judge, so to speak."

Don't have to use a simpler word for me, motherfucka. Who the fuck you think you are, man? Thaddeus contemplates tearing this motherfucka a new asshole for his patronizing ways. Cool it, man. Bitch Beverly digs this motherfucking shit. All life is selling. A master salesman uses any and all devices that come his way. Now if I seem to oil with this motherfucka, maybe she'll get off some pussy for a change. Beverly's been on strike since this whole credit card fight. Punishing me for her crimes. Jewboy rambling on . . . pay attention like you listening to Jesus on the Mount.

"I'd like you to consider me as more of an efficiency expert, someone brought in to an organization who is objective and tries to make things work better. For instance if you would give an example, without a characterizing label, of what you feel is inconsiderate about Thaddeus's behavior, that would give me a better idea . . ."

Beverly wants to say it serves him right she spends his money because he's such a damn braggart—talking about all that money he's going to make in the insurance business. What a big-shot salesman he's going to be. All those guys in that business talk about making big money and the manager slyly suggests at meetings and parties that it's up to the ladies to spend money and pile up debts so the boys will go out and hustle so she's only doing her job as a dutiful salesman's wife.

But she wants to seem a bit more demure than that—doesn't want this guy to think she's a gold digger or something. He doesn't have bad hair . . . curly and kinky, nice rich chestnut, and along with those heart-piercing blue eyes a real nice smile, though a bit forced and phony. She could make him smile for real. He speaks well—not put on like her husband. Does crosswords. Going to be a doctor. She'd be married to a Jewish doctor . . . maybe living next to Sheldon in Roslyn Heights. Watch his Barbara's ass get fatter through the years while her ass remains streamlined and sleek like the lines of a Jaguar. Sheldon sucking to get back with her. She dangles him in the wind.

"He keeps very late hours," she says. "I don't understand how one can be out selling policies till two or three in the morning with liquor on his breath."

Ah, a concrete issue. Jonathan nods but thinks of her, for a fleeting moment, at two o'clock in the morning, in bed and alone. In a shorty nightgown? He turns to Thaddeus for a reply. Thaddeus notes Beverly has taken on a pixieish air maybe to impress this motherfucka. She's got her little flirt machine going. They're setting up a real rapport. Motherfucka wants to get in her pants! I'll be a son of a bitch! Come to a goddamn Jew marriage counselor and first thing happens the Jew motherfucka wants to steal the black man's woman! Goddamn things never change, do they? They steal the gold out of your teeth and you ain't even dead yet. Steal your money every day in their stores and now this motherfucka lickin' his thick lips over my bitch.

Yet Thaddeus isn't really mad. His inner rhetoric doesn't resonate. Rather he's fascinated. Beverly is a copperhead and little Jewboy is a rabbit and the snake is circling the rabbit ready to snap rabbit's whole body into its wicked, slithering self and engulf it.

Thaddeus is perpetually cranky about his lot in life except when his beautiful little daughter smiles at him and sneaks in on his lap and cuddles him. Then all anger evaporates and the world is a beautiful place. She is his girl. He made her. He feels like a great artist, a builder—the Eiffel Tower, the Sistine Chapel. Yeah, man, I did that. He races home to pick her up from nursery school. He feeds her any chance he gets. He loves to take her into stores and spoil her rotten even though Bitch Beverly objects because he isn't spending his bread on her. She's daddy's little girl and Bitch Beverly doesn't like that. She tries to shield Janelle from her father. There's never anything overt in front of the kid—subtle shit—body language and attitude. She doesn't like him to be overly affectionate with Janelle—hug her, bounce her on his lap and stuff. She always there to somehow interfere. Once they had a fight about it and Bitch Beverly explained it's contrary to the way she was raised—Jamaicans aren't physically affection-ate with their kids—like the British. What they fear is child abuse—which is not uncommon in England but very rare in Jamaica; a case of the former captives becoming more civilized than their captors. Thaddeus is, if anything, physical. He's a hugger, grabber, toucher. He can't talk unless he's touching an arm or a shoulder, gets up close and makes you look him in the eye and get a whiff of his Clorets breath—(three packages a month at least). Janelle plays it too. Always jumping on him when her mother is nearby. Thaddeus is no one's fool. He sees the dynamic but his heart melts anyway. He wants to win his daughter over Bitch Beverly. His daughter is the only really good thing in his life.

"All right, at this point we have two very concrete situa-tions that have been brought out," Jonathan says before Thad-deus has a chance to respond to the charge of staying out all hours with liquor on his breath purportedly selling—which

Jonathan doesn't believe for a moment. Morris Schindler, the family insurance man, comes over early in the evening, transacts business with his father, and is out of the house—a cup of tea, not liquor, at eight thirty the latest. "I know both of you would like to respond to these situations here and now but I'd like you to hold on to your response until another session as we're almost out of time. Remember, we simply want to identify problem areas first and then we can outline a plan—a campaign, so to speak, that will address these issues with an idea toward resolving, reducing, and hopefully eliminating stressful, contentious patches in your life."

"I feel that is an excellent way to go about it," Beverly says, leaning back and tucking long, graceful fingers and perfectly manicured medium-length nails under her exquisite chin. Jonathan can't help *kvelling* because of her praise. Beverly moves her hand slowly up and down her amazingly swan-like neck.

"Well, our time is up," Jonathan mumbles, "unfortunately." His appointment book is ready. He has two openings in the morning later in the week. Thaddeus wants the first and gets it. Jonathan writes his name down. Beverly clocks how he writes. Slow and penmanship excellent. A man's character is in the way he writes. Not the thing you see in the papers where you can tell if someone is kind or dog-kicking nasty by the way they write their I or cross their t but in simple neatness and care about keeping to the line and forming words carefully no matter what the rush of events. Jonathan's fingers are stubby and she doesn't like that but his nails are clean. He writes with a real pen that makes a slight scratchy noise as it glides over the paper. She finds the noise enticing. She hates the way Thaddeus writes—quick, jerky, handwriting indecipherable and with a ballpoint pen. She could live with a man like Jonathan. He would carefully fold his own clothing and pick things up off the floor instead of flinging them down like her Teddy—she wishes she could get away with calling him that but he'd probably hit her.

So the first appointment—the opening shot—has been grabbed by her aggressive husband. She doesn't like that. He'll poison this nice gentleman against her. She'll have to counter his attacks. She wonders what she'll wear.

Chapter Two

Jonathan is seeing Arlene. They enjoy a communality of interests: career, foreign movies, modern jazz.

Arlene's the sexiest Jewish girl Jonathan has ever been with. A hand job on their first date, a blow job on the second (yes, can you believe it, a blow job from a Jewish girl and she knew what to do!). On the third date she went dutch (dutch!!) on a motel room. She came even before he did. With a new girl, Jonathan's clock time is around fifty-eight seconds after the head of his dick touches her labia. When he's a little used to the girl, he's good for almost two minutes. He recovers fast— maybe fifteen minutes . . . and then for the second time he can do maybe five minutes, which is normally enough for him to claim adequacy. Jonathan knew Arlene's orgasms weren't the usual Jewish girl fake because he could actually feel vaginal vibrations. His last girlfriend, Sheila, always claimed she came but he never believed her. Sheila was like a bad actress—a lot of huffing and puffing and shaking but no vaginal tremors like Arlene. Because of this Jonathan wonders if he ought to ask Arlene to marry him. But she's not all that pretty. Jonathan feels not all that handsome either, except maybe for the blue eyes which girls seem to like, so if he marries Arlene, his children are liable to be plain looking. Nobody in his family is really good looking so he feels he'd like to marry a really pretty woman (like Beverly but she's a *schvatza!* Oh, God) so he can have maybe two really gorgeous kids. It's a secret desire of his—so secret he's never told anyone, including Dr. Timothy Mitchell, his sacred, New Age shrink, who has been probing into his relationship with Arlene.

"Does she have them only when she's high?" Timothy asks this afternoon.

"No, not only then . . . she gets 'em all the time . . . when I play with her even before she smokes. I just touch and I feel like a tremor."

"Impressive."

"Yes."

"Have you ever been to Thailand?"

No one knows more about him than Timothy so why is he asking? Jonathan's hardly been off Long Island. He'd like to say that Timothy ought to know but he doesn't want to start up with him.

"In Bangkok I went to a sex show," Timothy says. "This beautiful Thai babe's able to open a coke bottle with her vagina. Then she puts a banana in there and squirts it like ten or fifteen feet up in the air. She has the muscles of her vagina trained."

"You think . . . ?"

"I'm only free-associating."

This is Timothy's technique. He free-associates with the client—none of this mask of objectivity for him. The meeting of unconscious minds as the most effective method of therapy. Jonathan knows as much about Timothy as Timothy knows about him. Timothy's attempting to spearhead a revival in the therapeutic community of R. D. Laing, the radical British shrink who was so popular in the sixties. Insanity is a sane reaction to an insane world. Jonathan can spout R. D. Laing with anyone, but secretly he scares him. Jonathan doesn't know if he wants to reach down or out to grasp certain segments of his personality. Sure there's a gorilla or tiger or eagle or something in all of us waiting to roar or whatever, but he would like to go through life happy, have good sex, cute kids, and enough money without waking any sleeping animals. Jonathan wants to seem on the verge of breaking loose, on the brink of grand self-discovery because he feels he has everything going for him except an edge. Any string of adjectives describing him would not include the one he truly longs for, edgy. Edgy is sexy. Girls will have sex with Jonathan not for the experience but for their future. He's not Marlon Brando in *Streetcar*, he's Karl Malden.

"You mean maybe Arlene has trained her muscles?" Jonathan asks.

"I suppose that's what I do mean. I suppose I'm suspicious."

"Why, just because she's Jewish? Isn't that bigoted? If she was say . . . African American, would you have had that association?"

Jonathan's pleased he's able to roll out African American. Jonathan, for the first time, the other night, used it to his family out in Merrick, Long Island.

His mother looked at him as if he was crazy and corrected him by saying, "You mean black, right?"

"No, African American, Mother."

"We go by continents now? Italian American is a country in a continent right? So if we want to be consistent why don't we get the country that the individual black comes from—like Rastus is Congo American and Leroy is Rwandan American."

"Those countries were not in existence when these people were brought over as slaves, Mother."

"I wish they'd make up their minds. For my parents, colored was okay—witness NAACP, which still remains—National Association for the Advancement of <u>Colored People</u>. Then Negro was good for us. It's still the Negro College Fund, isn't it? Black became beautiful when I was growing up but then when everyone was used to that they came up with African American. What next? Us, we were always Jews. We didn't feel we had to change our name to change people's perception of us. We came to America and they called us filthy Jews but now they call us filthy rich Jews. Let the blacks stay with whatever and let their accomplishments change their image rather than continually changing their name.

"You know I talk to Letty when she comes to clean and you know what I say, colored this and colored that, and she doesn't get upset one bit."

"How do you know she isn't seething with anger? One day she may cut your throat while you're napping," Jonathan said.

"That's disgusting!"

"Maybe I am bigoted," Timothy says. "I've never dated Jewish girls because of their reputation." Timothy is thirty-seven and has been married twice. He's from French-Canadian, Brit, Scotch background. He's swarthy as if he's from a coal-mining region in Pennsylvania or Ohio and has never gotten the soot out of his skin. He's living with a girl now—a full-blooded Indian girl from an upstate New York tribe. He's into pantheistic Indian culture but he complains his girl couldn't care less about that nature crap—can't stand looking at trees or grass—just give her plastic and fast cars. He sees it as a challenge to get her back to her native roots. They're probably on the verge of breaking up.

"I'm not suspicious of her sexiness," Jonathan says. "I'm surprised and . . ."

"And what?"

"Delighted."

"Delighted or . . . ?"

"What do you want me to say?"

Silence. Always silence when Jonathan says, what do you want me to say.

"Relieved," Jonathan says.

"Ahhh . . ."

"Well, okay, ahh . . . I found a Jewish girl who could have an orgasm. A real one. What's wrong with that?"

"Right or wrong has nothing to do with it. We're merely identifying patterns. In this case, your search."

"My search?"

"We all search. When you stop searching you stop living. We're not always aware, however, of what we are truly searching for."

"What do you mean?"

"Well, you've searched for a Jewish girl who is sexy and you found one. You desperately want to get married and out of the house and on your own. So what has stopped you from asking Arlene to marry you?"

"I don't know."

"Um-huh."

"She could be prettier."

"If you didn't find her pretty enough, why did you go with her in the first place?"

"She's not that bad. It started like a date. I didn't have anything else to do. I can't wait around for a Julia Roberts endlessly, can I? Turns out Arlene worships the sixties. Sex, drugs, and rock 'n' roll. She even has old hippie friends who've moved to Flushing and buy opium from Asians. I mean to me that's cool. Did you ever do opium?"

"Sure, in Thailand."

"How was it?"

"Great. I went on this trek up to the Hill Tribes in the Golden Triangle. You lie down, your head on a rock, right next to this kindly old guy who looks as if he's eighty but he's probably thirty-two—like opium wastes you, man. And he gently shows you how to do pipes. I did about six with him and I was off into paradise—the best ever . . ."

"Me too! This old hippie guy in Flushing did the same routine with me. At first I was scared and only did maybe two pipes and then increased it until I got up to ten and I got off and like the next morning I wake up and I've passed an eternity in pure bliss."

Jonathan loves telling about getting off on opium. He's told anyone and everyone in school, not at home of course. Opium is definitely edgy.

"I met Arlene in the student lounge at NYU. She's sitting there swearing like a sailor and showing daytime cleavage. Nighttime cleavage you're used to but daytime cleavage is startling. So I ask her out but it really wasn't her I was asking out, it was those things. I could hardly remember what Arlene looked like afterward. So she gives me her number and we're off. I never thought I'd be confronting a marriage decision. I figured in spite of the daytime cleavage and cussing and stuff she's like any Jewish girl. I'd have to sweat bullets before I finally got in her pants and then I'd have to worry about fending off the guilt-ridden marriage bullshit. Little did I know there'd not only be orgasmic sex but opium too. But with all that liberated shit she still wants to get married—I know it though she's never come right out and admitted it."

"Well, if she did, what would you do?"

"I don't know. I'm afraid I'd cave in and marry her."

"Cave in?"

"I have all these horrible middle-class thoughts. She's making a decent salary. I'm going to get my doctorate and start making good money. My father promised me a down payment on a starter home when I marry. I'm off and running on my life and it should be a good life. Just the way I was brought up except my ideas are like stultifying, life choking. There's no liberation to them. No joy. No vivacity. I understand all that but the tug is still there. I don't know what to do—which way to turn. Like Arlene might be perfect for me because we have the same kinds of conflicts although she doesn't seem to worry about it as much as I do. She seems like a real free spirit."

"Let your life be middle class but your mind totally liberated. I paraphrase Flaubert."

"Wasn't he somewhat of a passive-aggressive depressive?"

"It seems that way."

"You can't get me a better source for a good quote like that?"

When the session's over, Jonathan thinks if he ever made love to anyone like Beverly—never mind anyone like Beverly . . . say Beverly . . . and her pussy vibrated would he doubt, for one moment, she was for real.

It hits Beverly. What it is about Jonathan. He looks like the guy on the American Express card. Same profile, same nose. Beverly obsesses about credit cards. It's not so much what they buy, it's the method. When she was growing up in Jamaica you had to have money to buy something or you couldn't get it. Credit was only for mortgages on property. You needed cash in stores or you didn't buy. She came to America when she was fourteen and by the time she was eighteen, out of high school and working in lower Manhattan for Paine Webber and going to college at night for hotel management, she had her own credit card. She's in awe of them but she's been accustomed to only going halfway. The charging half not the paying back half. When she was single she gave her paycheck to her mother who then paid the credit card. When she married, at first Thaddeus paid the credit card but then when he became too much of a big shot to be bothered with such things, he gave the task to her and she simply didn't do it.

Her first real boyfriend—not counting guys she let grope her while no one was home but a guy who took her to the movies and out dancing—was a Jamaican guy named Trevor who was in his midtwenties and had just gotten a job with the transit authority. Trevor refused to own a credit card claiming it led to fiscal irresponsibility. He annoyed her when he whipped out cash to pay for a meal in a restaurant that had credit card signs displayed. Their relationship didn't last very long. Beverly didn't want any of these old-fashioned, tight-ass Jamaican guys. Sheldon Goldblatt always had a credit card somewhere on his person and he used it wherever and whenever he could. His parents were always yelling at him for the outrageous bills he ran up but they paid the bills and never deprived him of the credit card.

When you came down to it, Thaddeus had really gotten her to marry him under a false premise. The fact she'd gotten pregnant with him really didn't make any difference. She could have gotten rid of that baby in a flash and gone on about her way but for one thing. Thaddeus had an American Express card. She first met him in an upscale Caribbean restaurant in the city while having dinner with her girlfriend Thelma before they were to go clubbing. Thaddeus came over because he'd met Thelma before, sat down real pushy and started that close talk of his, but when the check came he whipped out this card with that cute picture of this guy with a Jewish nose in a Roman helmet and her heart fluttered because it was American

Express Gold. This guy, Thaddeus, held in that too-dark paw of his the means to do anything at anytime—buy anything no matter how much it cost. American Express Gold—no limit. Tiffany's, Cartier's, Bergdorf, a trip to the Greek Isles, Paris.

Thaddeus wasn't any damn insurance peddler then. He claimed he was in automotives, specializing in customized, luxury sports vehicles. She found out when it was too late he was a damn used car salesman on Queens Boulevard in Kew Gardens but that first night all she could focus on was that American Express Gold tucked neatly into the fold of his flat wallet. So after they married, Thaddeus gave up the American Express and got himself a no-fee Visa with a credit limit. When she found out about what he'd done, it was as if her life foundation collapsed. She felt trapped and betrayed, so instead of really trying to work out the weird relationship she found herself locked into—a mother and wife to a man she really oughtn't to spend five minutes with . . . —she became bitter and detached.

Beverly is aware of how she feels but doesn't want anyone else to know it, especially this marriage counselor, because she knows she's being immature. She didn't originate this marriage counseling business to get reprimanded and then possibly deprived of her credit card. She can't live with Thaddeus without one—okay no more American Express Gold, she's reconciled to that like a kid who finally knows there's no Santa Claus, but at least a Visa with a pretty high limit. Hell, all that fool has to do each and every month is pay off the minimum balance and no one will bother you. She should have done that but didn't. Now, she supposes, if she stays married, she's going to have to.

She thinks about Jonathan and can't help wondering if he has a credit card and how she could find out. She really finds him sort of attractive in a goofy way. White guys can be goofy and still cute but black guys ought to be real handsome because they got all that dark skin and kinky hair against them.

"Well, what you think?" Thaddeus asks her as they're driving home from the marriage counseling session.

"About what?"

"About what do you think you think you ought to be thinking about?"

"You suppose to be telling me what I ought to be thinking about?"

Thaddeus, pissed, veers a hard right onto the street where they live.

"Beverly, we are going through an ordeal," Thaddeus says, trying to be patient. Beverly feels her hackles rising. "We are baring our souls to a man we don't even know—a white man no less . . ."

"I don't see what the man's color has to do with it," Beverly says testily. "I feel no sense of alienation from any race— much less the white race."

They'd gone over this before. American blacks are all hung up with this slavery thing. Jamaicans are more comfortable with race because they don't have that horrible history as a burden. Thaddeus wishes Beverly might try to understand but she's deliberately obdurate.

They pass some scroungy drug dealers hanging out just a few doors away from their little house. "Look at those fools," Beverly says sharply. "You can't do nothing about that, can you? We have to raise Janelle with the dope heads."

"If you didn't spend all my money, we could save to get out of here. If you want a down payment on a house in Long Island so we can get away from all this trash around here, then I need domestic tranquility. I cannot focus on selling.

Do you understand that, woman? If I can't focus on selling we have to stay where we are."

Beverly doesn't want to stay where she is. She only has a short period of time left to attract a really good man who could take her away from all this. She doesn't think she ought to waste it with this fool but she has very little alternative except to live with her parents but they get on her nerves almost as much as her fool husband. Her options are limited. Maybe she ought to make do with this one since she's been dumb enough to have a baby with him. But the thought depresses her. Shouldn't life be better? Especially since she's gifted with looks. What a waste. She has a cousin Grace, absolutely beautiful when young, married a drunk who beat her and then left her when she was old and drained. Everyone talks about how beautiful she'd been. Is she going to be that way? A couple of times Thaddeus has come close to hitting her. And his staying out all hours. He certainly is out there chasing. Why should she stand for it?

If Jonathan's pants were off she could sneak a look in his wallet. She's certain she'd find American Express Gold.

Thaddeus idly thinks about the information gleaned on the brochure about the Jamaica Family Center—Family Counseling, Drug Rehabilitation, and Alcohol Abuse Rehabilitation. They got summer camp for children who have never seen trees that don't get pissed against by dope heads—music therapy, art therapy, therapy therapy. All great stuff, brought to us poor black folks who never knew we'd been yearning for this kind of shit by . . . New York State, grants from the Feds through the Department of Social Services, and . . . yes . . . Jewish Philanthropies, the United Jewish Way as well all those charitable institutions you try to avoid at the office when some motherfucka hits you for a dollar. Just yesterday at the office Joe Kahn told him a joke about this big clothing

manufacturer who gets up at a convention of Jewish Philanthropies, puffs on his cigar and says, "I'm Irving Finklestein,
Finklestein Bras Incorporated—1414 Seventh Avenue—and I
hereby donate two million dollars. Anonymously." Thaddeus
laughed then reflected the joke would never work with a black
millionaire because no one'd imagine such a creature existed.

Thaddeus thinks about the way Mr. I Ain't No Doctor Yet
Jonathan Meltzer looked at Bitch Beverly. Thaddeus knows a
fuck look from a guy when he sees one. Then it hits him. The
formula. Shit, he always was good at math.

M+DP=HT. Malpractice + Deep Pockets=Happy Thaddeus.

Come to the white man for help, he wind up fucking
my wife! Breaking up my home. Leaving me a broken man!
Making a damn adulteress out of the mother of my child! Big
bucks in a settlement. Get custody of Janelle. Her mother's
a whore, your honor. My daughter needs to be raised in a
moral, upstanding home. Then he thinks about Maureen at
the office. Been circling Maureen and she been circling him.
They held on to each other a little bit just yesterday by the
copying machine. He snatched her hand and she tried to break
away. "Cut it out," she whispered. He didn't want to come
on too strong so he let go but just before she turned and
left she squeezed his hand and shot him a look that sent his
dick rising. Then his sales manager, the Colonel, walked by,
knew what was happening—what was beginning to happen
anyway. The Colonel didn't approve. The Colonel liked to nail
the office girls first before he let any of the other guys have
them and he hadn't nailed Maureen because Maureen didn't
dig him.

Thaddeus doesn't really know how he'd feel if someone
touched Bitch Beverly. She a bitch all right, but she my bitch.
Man ain't supposed to let anyone else handle his own wife
even for a million dollar settlement.

Would a Jew trade his bitch in for big bucks? Shit, most of those guys at the office would trade theirs in for a couple of new shirts if they could get someone to take them off their hands. That's why the Jews're rich cause they don't worry about outmoded ideas of manhood. You go fight in Vietnam, motherfucka, while I get my ass in the Coast Guard or sneak off to Canada or stay in college till the cows come home. It's the black man gets his manly balls shot off. The Jewboy trade his own mother for a pot of gold. If I'm going to get anywhere in this motherfucking world I'd better start thinking and acting like a goddamn Jew. Jew got an asset he maximize it. Lookit Bitch Beverly. That is my golden cigar! Bitch lookin' to dump me anyway is why she gets my ass to this counseling shit so she can say she did all she could to "save the marriage." I know that bitch. She wants to trade me in while she still foxy. Get herself a cushier deal. Take my daughter away from me. Make me a Sunday daddy.

Car gets parked in front of their stingy little home on their shoddy-housed, narrow street. The only thing decent about their house is the landscaping, which Thaddeus takes pride in and does himself. Beverly swings the gate back at Thaddeus in annoyance, hoping it gets him in the crotch. Thaddeus catches it before it does damage. Beverly glares at a loose shutter that needs fixing on the bedroom window. When it's windy it makes noise keeping her awake. Thaddeus ignores her glare. He could fix that damn shutter in a minute but fuck her—he's a sound sleeper so it doesn't keep him up. Besides, if he did fix it he'd be like any other damn nigger around here doing his own housework. Gardening and land-scaping is different—that's almost like art, some of these great millionaires love to do their own gardening but hammering, sawing, and painting is guinea shit. Sy Silverstein don't do shit around the house—calls him a guinea if anything needs fixing. Shit, I'd like to have me a guinea.

Chapter Three

"Can I be perfectly honest with you?" Thaddeus asks.

"That is exactly what we need—perfect honesty," Jonathan replies. He leans back and puts his hands on the back of his head. Thaddeus debates with himself. Then:

"Man, this isn't what I was going to say but I got to give you a little tip. This shit must go." Thaddeus imitates Jonathan.

"Body language, man," Thaddeus says. "That's what we learn in selling. What are you telling me when you lean back and put your hands on your head like that?"

"I don't know. What?"

"You are threatened and you wish to be uninvolved. You are putting yourself miles away from the proceedings. You are asking the other party to . . . entertain you . . . as if you are a pasha or something. Get it?"

Thaddeus is leaning across the desk. Jonathan is leaning so far back now he's afraid he's going to tumble backward and fall on his neck. He doesn't know what to do. Should he immediately change his position because perhaps the client is correct or should he maintain control and go into the client's motives for this attack? No wonder this guy is having marriage problems, he's so damn aggressive but then he castigates himself for evolving into judgment simply because the client is honest. Would he feel this way if the client's wife were a dog?

"Now you've put me in an awkward situation," he tells Thaddeus. "If I immediately remove my hands and change my posture I'm allowing you to control these proceedings and there's a bit of a danger there." Jonathan feels good. He's being clever. "If I do not, I stand a chance you'll think me obdurate . . . I mean stubborn . . ."

"I know what obdurate means." Thaddeus's eyes flash anger briefly. "I'm only trying to be helpful," Thaddeus explains reasonably. "You see you and me are in the same boat, so to speak. We have to be out there in front of the public doing our thing . . . you know what I mean? Maybe you have a great deal of training but you too young to have a great deal of experience. Me, I've been selling since I was fourteen years old. I hustled everything except dope—never got involved with anything downright illegal but maybe once in a while a little bit shady—like magazines never got delivered, watches with tick bugs inside, stocks that didn't exist, cars that didn't run after they got out of the lot, real estate in Florida had crocodiles on it. You name it I sold it. But I wanted something respectable so I wound up in the insurance business—everything on the up and up there except we bullshit the public like crazy. We make a life insurance policy everything but a life insurance policy. It gets to be a razzle-dazzle investment plan. It gets to be your Gateway to Heaven. It gets to be peace of mind and retirement in sunny Florida. Sell the sizzle not the steak . . . know what I mean? I don't mind telling you all this cause everything strictly confidential, right?"

"Right." Jonathan sneaks his hands down slowly. He's changed positions without compromising himself. Thaddeus doesn't seem to notice. The subject's dropped. Jonathan's pleased to have finessed himself out of the situation. Dr. Timothy Mitchell sometimes adopts the same posture—particularly at the beginning of the session. Jonathan can't wait to zing it to him next time he does it.

"Now here's what I want to be honest about," Thaddeus says. "I got a problem with women. I got to bear my soul to you right?"

"Right."

"This way we get to the root of my problem with women in general, you know what I mean?"

"Of course." Jonathan is on a mental roller coaster ride. He doesn't particularly like Mr. Thaddeus Carmichael but there is something about all this energy and the surprising, even startling way his mind works that is beginning to mesmerize him in a vaguely admiring way.

"Like chicks make no bones about liking to fuck . . . not like the old days. Carry condoms on 'em in case you forget. Know how to slip 'em on too . . . like rip, out of the tin, unfold, over the head and down the shaft in one smooth motion. Right?

"I know you can't comment on shit like that because you got to appear above the fray—full of no sexual feelings sagacity, right? I know how this therapy shit comes down. You get a hard-on, you supposed to analyze it. I dig. But no shit, I mean the way I think of chicks is like they're sex objects. You think if my bitch wasn't foxy I'd put up with half her shit? She's a sex object."

She certainly is, Jonathan thinks.

"But that's wrong," Thaddeus asserts. "I been wrong all my life and look what it's brought me to. I never should have married that woman."

"You regret it?"

"Hell yeah. No matter how foxy a bitch is when she your wife, she your wife. I mean when that woman was my girl-friend . . . shit . . ." Thaddeus lapses into a sigh and a far-away look as if he's flashing back to a lovingly amorous age beyond words. Jonathan images Beverly on an ethereal bed-cloud, writhing sensually before he shuts that particular image down so he can concentrate.

"I don't even want to think about that compared to . . . now," There's almost a sob in Thaddeus's voice.

Jonathan would like to ask him to go into detail but he suspects his motive is akin to a kid wanting to know some hot sexual details. He doesn't ask anything. He waits.

"Now I got to plead for pussy," Thaddeus complains. "The garbage got to go out. I got to shower. I got to have been well behaved all day. I come into the bedroom, she tucked under the cover with her nightie on. I try to make some moves, warm her up, but she says, 'Get on with it, man.' Treat me like a Saturday night whore. Half the time I can't even come fucking her as my wife so I have to think about the way I used to fuck her as my girlfriend. Dig? I mean it's getting to be like one of those Jewish marriages I hear these guys in the office complain about. No offense now, man, okay."

"Of course, in therapy you can say anything that comes to mind."

"These guys get pussy from their women by the day of the week. Like Saturday night out there in suburbia is when the ladies pull their car up to your pump."

Jonathan thinks about his father—yeah if he's lucky.

"You ain't gonna bring up anything you learn from me to her, do you?" Thaddeus asks.

"Of course not."

"If I was to tell you about the life I really lead I wouldn't be getting into trouble with my wife, would I?"

"Everything you tell me is confidential. I will only use the material that we both agree on in joint sessions. You may rely on that."

"I got to trust you now, man, right?"

"Of course."

"I mean she ain't the only duck in my pond, you know what I mean?"

"Okay, but let me ask you something. If you don't care about the relationship, regret getting married and all that, why should you care if she finds out? Might be your way out, right?"

"You one smart man." Thaddeus wanted to say one smart Jewboy but refrained. That's what he likes about Jews. They're smart—greedy and shit but smart. So this nerdy little Jewboy is really smart too like the rest of his breed. Good, no Jew worse than a dumb one though they're hard to find. Thaddeus beams his brights at Jonathan. Jonathan beams back. They've overcome some hurdle.

"Listen, man, I really love my daughter. I don't want her hating me cause I abandoned her. I don't want my wife to poison that child's heart against me. That's why I want to keep things going. That girl is my life. Dig?"

"Wouldn't it be in the best interest of your daughter . . . what's her name by the way?"

"Janelle."

"Ah, pretty . . . anyway wouldn't it be in Janelle's best interest to grow up in a harmonious home? You know children are deeply affected by the conflicts of their parents."

"You so right. That's why I'm here. For her sake."

"Children sense when there's no real harmony. The whole idea of staying together for the children's sake is being rethought, so to speak, by society at large."

"Are you suggesting I divorce my wife?"

"Of course not, I'm here to help your marriage work but for the right reasons. I wonder if staying together so that one parent doesn't poison the other to the child is a strong enough bond for a continuing marriage."

"Hey, man, you talking some real shit. I never thought of that."

"Any relationship built only on a sense of duty is bound to be filled with resentment and anger. Don't you agree?"

"Yeah, of course."

"Well, then our job is to build your relationship with your family on more solid emotional grounds. You're both, at this point, obviously filled with anger and resentment at each other—that's what brought you here. If we can resolve the problems that led to those feelings you can go back to the wonderful things that led you to get together to begin with."

"You know what the wonderful thing that was the bedrock of our relationship? Her looks. Don't ask me about what she was about—say as a person. If I thought about that at all I'd have run for the motherfucking hills. I seen her at this place with her girlfriend Thelma who I used to fuck in my car when she couldn't get a ride home. Bitch too cheap to take a taxi. I went over and made a big play for Beverly and she was paying me no mind at all until I whipped out my credit card . . . bet you thought I was going to say my dick . . . and paid for dinner for her and Thelma. Well, then Beverly all over me. Where I buy my suits? Oh you so sharp and how many Porsches I own? I feed her so much bullshit you'd think she'd choke on it but she couldn't get enough. Shit by the time the night was over my net worth exceeded the Rockefellers'. Well, naturally I couldn't take her to my seedy apartment so I checked into a fancy New York hotel, like $300 a room, and while I'm fucking her she wants to hear more about like where I go on vacation and shit and how much I spend at the roulette wheels when I go to Monte Carlo . . . shit I never been near no Monte Carlo. Well the more I piled it on, the wetter her pussy got. I couldn't believe it. That bitch, when she gets going, when she thinks she's on the money bed, can buck with the best of them. Bitch ought to be a whore.

"So now the night's over and I figure shit what a good time I had. Spent big bucks but sure got my money's worth. Oh hum on to the next challenge except now Beverly on the phone wanting to see me again. ASAP. Well shit I can't keep up that pace. That damn night cost me over $400. What to do? I make a date with her to meet her in a cool lounge in Manhattan—I pick gay in Chelsea because gay is in these days. She come in glowing and gorgeous and we sit and have a drink and before I know it her hand up my leg playing with my joint and I figure, shit I got me an American Express credit card with no limit so what the fuck. You only live once. Girls look like Beverly don't come around that much, you know what I mean?"

Jonathan knows what he means. He's always admired anyone with American Express because they can do anything they want. No limit. He wonders if Dr. Timothy Mitchell has American Express. Someone once told Jonathan he looked like that Roman soldier on the card. What if he's in a restaurant with a girl who looks like Beverly—looks like bullshit . . . what if he's in a restaurant with Beverly and he hands out a Visa to pay for the stuff and the waiter comes back and says, I'm sorry sir you've exceeded your limit. Crushing. With American Express you can never have that happen to you.

"Well then me and Beverly go on a spree," Thaddeus says. "I forget all about the fact that while you can charge anything you want on American Express you also got to pay it back and if you don't pay off the full balance at the end of the month they rap you with a big motherfucking interest rate and you are on your way to serious trouble. But who cares? We go to the best places to dance and drink. I sneak the best cars off the lot to chauffeur her around in. I tell her they all mine and man I'm telling you we had the best time I ever had in my life. We struttin' our stuff. We doin' our thing. The sky is the limit. But then she unloads on me. She's pregnant.

"The sky now falls in on me, man. I'm in debt up to my ears. I get fired cause they find out I been taking different cars out every night to see Beverly. Beverly tells me I don't have to marry her if I don't want to. Island women used to getting knocked up and not getting married but if I don't marry her she never wants to see me again and she'll take care of raising the kid her own self. By this time she is planted deep under my skin but I don't want to get married. I'm afraid. Been leading the good life. Wine, women, and song and now I got no job, no credit worth a shit, and a baby on the way and marriage facing me or I lose the prettiest bitch I ever seen. What do I do? I give in, that's what I do. That woman got her claws in me. But before I do I sit her down and confess. I tell her everything about me. The real two-face double-crossing lying-ass me."

"What happens then?"

"She doesn't believe me. She thinks I'm trying to weasel out of getting married. I have to prove what a lowlife I am so I run home and get those nasty letters they send you when you don't pay and she finally believes me."

"And . . . ?"

"She tells me to get out and don't let the door hit my ass as I go. Woman turned ugly like you never seen. Looked like a witch of Salem—you know the Jamaican one got burned along with all the little white girls and shit . . ."

"Then what happened?"

"I got religion."

"Religion?"

"I was moping around, calling her, trying to win a little more pussy before she dumps me completely and then an old buddy of mine shows up at my doorstep—ol' Vincent Beauford. Me and him used to hustle watches on Forty-Second Street—he shill for me and I shill for him and we made some good bucks—then go out and party and shit, get broke and be out hustling the next day. Beauford got him a nice suit and tie and he driving a Mercedes he claims he owns outright. I'm impressed. He's a life insurance salesman only now they call it a financial planner and before I could laugh him out the door he tells me how much legit money you can make in that business and you are working for the up and up of America. Meridian Life Insurance Company. You are like a minister of the Lord pounding the bible. Widows and children. Respectable yet lucrative. Ol' Vince married and buying a house out in Brentwood, Long Island—corner lot, Colonial white columns like the slave owners used to have on a cul-de-motherfucking-sac! He brings me into his office and sits me down with one of the most amazing cats I ever met—he's this big, black retired army colonel and he's the fucking manager of this whole big office—Jewish life insurance agents and black agents. The dream is here and now. The sky is the limit to what you can earn! Nobody can take shit away from you. Cops can't chase you. Boss can't fire you or cut up your territory. You selling security not empty watches with little tick bugs in 'em. Dig? Widows and children and old folks . . . I get fired up and go to Beverly with my new religion and I tell her I got something better than a damn American Express. I got a real no limit. I can make tons of money and I want to marry her and bring up our child and move our ass out to Long Island and buy our own plantation colonial—have guinea gardeners as our slaves. Man I tell you one thing I can do when I put my mind to it. I can sell. I can sell like a motherfucka and I'm talking to her for like two minutes telling her about all I'm going to do for her and our little baby growing underneath that sweet little belly button of hers and her eyes glistening and her mouth watering and she says yes . . . yes a thousand times yes and then she gets off some of the best pussy ever in the saga of pussydom. Man, I can just remember it as I'm talking about it."

He sure can sell, Jonathan thinks. Thaddeus is glowing, he's jumping in his seat, he's sweating and gesticulating. Jonathan admires it. Jonathan can't get so excited about anything—a woman, a career . . . whatever. He regrets it yet is comforted because he'll come out all right where a guy like Thaddeus will probably wind up in deep shit. Would he consider a trade—his emotional life for Thaddeus's? Sure but only safely—a no-harm guarantee. His life is going that way but would he ever make love to a woman who looks like Beverly?

"What is it you want—now from your marriage?" Jonathan asks.

"I want her to appreciate me. I want her to value my work. Me! I'm out there busting my ass for my family. Oh, sure I ain't made the big bucks yet. I'm going to be a great success but it takes time and I need to have a woman in my corner instead of her being the fighter who gets up as my opponent when the bell rings. Dig?"

"How can she show you she's in your corner?"

"She can stop putting me down all the time. She can get up off some pussy. She can stop spending all my money. That would be great for openers."

"And what could you do as far as her complaints about you are concerned?"

"Like?"

"Late hours."

"If she nice to me I'll come home when I ought to. I'm out there chasing what I ought to be having right there in my home. I'm knocking on some pussy's door that don't hold a motherfucka candle to the pussy I got at home. Now does that make sense? Would I do that if I didn't need what any man needs but I ain't gettin? You dig?"

"I dig."

They smile at each other. Connecting for the first time on a man-to-man basis. Jonathan holds on to his objectivity, realizing Thaddeus is seductive, treating him like a buddy in a bar and Jonathan almost succumbing.

Jonathan realizes Thaddeus has created a rejecting world that he can feel comfortable railing against and rebelling from. At this stage in his life Beverly is the engine that enables him to drive his neurosis this way and that. He plays victim to manipulate without really being concerned about the consequences of his manipulation—almost like a sociopath. He can evoke warm, compelling images—love and devotion to daughter and a desire to be a success for his family. Rather than being sincere motivations, they are merely subterfuges to continuously spin the top of his neurosis.

"Would you like me to be sympathetic with your need to find other . . . sexual relationships outside of your marriage?" Jonathan asks.

Thaddeus is thrown off-stride with that one. "Can't you see . . . what I'm up against?" he mumbles.

"You'd like me to see you as . . . a victim of some kind?"

"No . . . no of course not . . . we all make our own worlds, don't we?"

"Is that what you really believe?"

"Yeah."

"Um-huh."

"What is it you want me to say?"

"Only what comes to mind . . . anything that comes to mind."

"I feel you're being hard on me, like I opened up to you and you're judging me."

"I'm not here to judge you but to help you. You said you wanted to get over your problem with women, right?"

"Yeah, I do."

"Was that something you feel I might be pleased to hear because I'm a therapist or do you really want to get over your problem with women?"

Thaddeus thinks about Maureen. Yeah, maybe get free of some of my shit and be with her in the right way. But the thought scares him, catches him off guard so he can't say that. Jonathan leans forward sensing vulnerability.

"What comes to mind now?" Jonathan asks.

"Nothing. Nothing."

Thaddeus is hiding something—out with it, damn it. Some weird anger has come over Jonathan.

"I think our time is up now," Jonathan says, glancing at his watch after he says it. There're actually three minutes left. Thaddeus sneaks a quick look at his watch and notices the same three minutes.

Son of a bitch got himself in an uproar, Thaddeus thinks. He's real pissed off at me. Thaddeus likes it. He beams a big one at Jonathan, takes his hand in his, covers it with his free hand and right in the eye says, "Thank you very much, Jonathan. I feel this has been a most productive session, don't you?"

Jonathan's disoriented. He'd like to say wait we have three minutes left; I made a mistake. But therapists don't make mistakes, they only make faulty countertransference adjustments. He called the session off early because . . . oh shit he doesn't know why except this guy pisses him off. And the guy knows it. Thaddeus grips the door handle before Jonathan can and leaves.

Jonathan feels bested.

"Mrs. Carmichael . . ."

"I thought we were going to be on a first-name basis," Beverly says demurely. She's wearing a simple print dress cut slightly above the knee. She crosses her legs so there's a deep wedge of sepia thigh readily visible. He can tell she's taken some care with her makeup and clothes. Shoe color coordinated with bag, dress, and makeup. He's scared. He hadn't mentioned her at his session with Timothy. He'll wait until he sees how this session goes in case his conflicts resolve and there'll be no need. Yet doubt gnaws. He's fucking up by not talking about it to his therapist. He's too guarded, playing too safe, protecting himself, as always. He knows it but doesn't want to hear it from his therapist because then his therapist will use it on him to prod and disturb him in future sessions.

"Remember with this Beverly thing when you yourself said you were being too guarded?" But he's perpetuating his problem by being too guarded. Look at Thaddeus—so frank. Except for that screwed-up ending they'd had a wonderful initial session and because of it Jonathan feels now he'll be able to help him. He should use Thaddeus as an example. But there's something demeaning about that. Thaddeus is the client and he's the therapist. There's a trace of race too which he doesn't want to acknowledge. He's supposed to be of a higher order, isn't he? He really feels that though he's clearly liberal. These people can't be blamed for their baser instincts because of what they've been through. He can still be a liberal and recognize their limitations. There's a bit of a cognitive dissonance in that but no essential dichotomy.

"Of course," he says, throat dry. "Beverly . . ."

"Jonathan," she says as if trying out a new flavor at Baskin-Robbins and liking the taste. "Jonathan," she says again as if then ordering a cone with two scoops and whipped cream on top. "We like names with many syllables. By we, I mean Jamaicans. It's silly I know, but it's almost as if the more syllables in a name the more important you are as a person. Americans, I don't believe, care about such things. You are all Bills and Bobs. Your presidents are Dick and Jack and there was Ike. Your democracy makes everyone common. We have a democracy too but still reserve the right to, at least, sound exalted."

Jonathan is disoriented. Where did this come from? Is he really in crime-poverty Jamaica, Queens, on a dingy elevated subway street, ministering therapy to the poor, barely literate or is he on the set of a George Bernard Shaw play? This Beverly is supposed to be a common little Jamaican immigrant too easily persuaded by the glint of a man's credit card and she suddenly has a command of language and ideas that would impress an English professor.

"Well, now that we are here, tell me, what am I supposed to do?" she asks somewhat disingenuously. "Oh, supposed to talk about my husband. Complain about him, is that right?"

"You may say what you like. You don't have to complain about your husband if you don't want to."

Sheldon loved it when she talked about her "hang-ups" as he called them so . . . "For some reason I'd like to speak more about . . . me. Is that all right?"

"Yes."

"I've thought about my problems. I haven't always done the right thing. I've really been too impressed with material things. I realize that now because I see where it has gotten me in my life. Sometimes I wake up in the middle of the night—nights when he's home, shocked that a creature like this sleeps besides me, is my husband, me the mother of his child. I allowed myself to be taken in by his big talk because I was . . . or maybe I should say am . . . because maybe I haven't gotten over it yet even though I know I should . . . I am greedy. Greed is like a boomerang, it returns and hits you in the face. I don't like that in myself."

Jonathan can hardly breathe. He never expected this kind of analytical, perceptive confession. She talks in a lilting voice. Even when she comes to her sin—greed—she says the word softly caressing yet repudiating at the same time, her voice and manner expressing her conflict.

"Can you help me overcome this?" she looks at him plaintively. "And now is the first time I've ever said this either out loud or to myself. This problem I have. This . . . greed."

"Of course I can help you." He leans forward, fully committed to her.

Beverly stands and moves to the wall and studies a picture of a thoroughly pedestrian landscape. Jonathan can't help noticing how tall she is—almost as tall as he is. Her leg briefly touches an old, green studio couch that rests against the wall. For a moment he's afraid she's going to sit on it, lean back, and strike some seductive pose but she studies the picture for a few seconds and then turns to him full face.

"This marriage will take care of itself," she says. "It will stand or fall on its own. I have a daughter. I do not want her to make the same mistake as her mother. I want to replace this shallow set of values I have with values of more substance. This, I know, is not easy. I am like an alcoholic. I walk down the street and if a store displays a credit card sign—especially, oh my goodness I find myself able to talk to you . . . tell you all my secrets . . ."

A tingle up and down his spine. The way she looks at him when she says that—eyes open, lips slightly parted, she leans on the desk and then sits down. He needs to get more of a grip on what is really happening here. Is she playing him? Trying to make herself seem more deserving of his therapeutic skills than her husband? Of course she is.

"Especially . . . an American Express credit card. I get a little obsessed. It's wrong I know but the impulses are there. Even coming here this morning. I dropped Janelle off at my mother's early and walked around Jamaica Avenue. There's a new clothing store and I looked at the window not to see what they are displaying but to check out if they honor American Express. They do. I feel like hanging out to see who pays with American Express. If it's a man I think maybe . . . I'll flirt with him . . . develop a romance or something. Of course I would never do this . . . it's like a fantasy . . ."

"Yes, of course, you know in therapy we deal in fantasies . . ."

"I know that," she snaps a bit—but good-humoredly. She's caught him being patronizing but she's not all that mad. It's like a little boy doing a mildly wrong thing. Who said she was a harridan?! "That's why I'm telling them to you. I wouldn't tell my fantasies to my eye doctor or to my gynecologist."

He wonders if this reference to her gynecologist is at all suggestive. He's aware of perspiration trickling down his armpits. He's afraid there might be some on his upper lip. He ought to grow a therapist's beard—make him look older and wiser. He definitely is going to lose weight and get in better shape.

"What do you think the origins of this problem are?" he asks, glad his voice is neutral.

"I think it's my mother. She's very grasping, you know. My father is a hard-working carpenter—a simple man but good . . . doesn't fool around . . . home on time, that kind of thing . . . but my mother has never appreciated him. She has always felt she married beneath her. She's a beautiful woman and well educated too but by the time she was in her early twenties she was raising three children so now she feels life has passed her by. I feel the same way too. I vowed never to be like her and wound up being just like her—same resentments, same feelings about my husband, same desire to see to it that my daughter doesn't turn out that way too. And my answer has been greed. But it's so stupid. Even when I buy something now the pleasure is short-lived because underneath I know the reason for my purchase is not good. Yet knowing this I do it anyway."

"When did you come to this realization?"

"Oh, I've really always sort of had it. Always knew my life was heading the wrong direction even as I headed it there. Isn't that peculiar?"

"Not as much as you think. It's actually sort of common."

"I never spoke about it before—never wanted to admit it out loud. In some sense I now realize I ignored those credit card letters in order to create a family crisis so I could get Thaddeus and me to counseling so I could wind up admitting my problem to a therapist to try to resolve it."

Jonathan's amazed at this degree of sophisticated perception. The entire methodology of neurotic acting out at her fingertips without having to crack one textbook or get bored by one tiresome lecture.

What an amazing couple they are, this Thaddeus and Beverly. He must force himself to talk about them to Timothy.

"Of course I wonder now that I've admitted these things to you how you will handle this information," Beverly says.

"You mean as far as . . . ?"

"Yes, Thaddeus . . . or . . ." she smiles mischievously. He's seen a smile like that in the centerfold of *Playboy* just this month on the face of Miss April—when he looked at her face. Miss April is not black or even near brown. She's a big blonde from Kansas with nipples the size of coffee saucers but the way her mouth does this little Cheshire is exactly the same as Beverly now. "Teddy . . . oh yes, may I say it again?"

Jonathan nods.

"Teddy! Teddy! Oh God I have wished to say that so long! Teddy! Ted!! You sure you're not going to tell him any of this?"

"No."

"Teddy!!!!" she shouts.

Jonathan for a moment thinks about quieting her. The walls are thin. Someone is liable to think . . . think what? Why is he so scared? So guarded? Fuck 'em. Let her shout all she wants.

"I hate that name!"

Jonathan gazes up at her passionate flushed face and realizes for the first time in his life he's in love.

In love!

Beverly waits for his comments. He must speak. But he doesn't quite know what to say. He uses silence, the therapist's most reliable bulwark against communication. He now realizes with the force of a body slam that he's never really been in love before. She has a beachhead on his soul. He wishes he could now lean toward her and tell her how he feels about her and devil take the hindmost. From here on in, he knows, everything is a charade. He doesn't know how he's going to handle this.

Beverly is stunned by her own performance. She came here convinced she wasn't simply going to harp on and on about Thaddeus. Any fool who listened to Thaddeus more than three seconds could see why any woman worth her salt would have problems with him. Why waste time? She isn't going to show herself as a common little Queens housewife complaining about her common life-insurance-peddler husband. She's allowed herself to simply say what's on her mind no matter what—maybe to impress this nice man. She longs for the world to see the real her. Educated, with fine qualities, lost for now but not entirely diminished. She simply wants to be her real, finest self. Her old boyfriend had the answer. When she was with him she had it too. Free and joyous. No restrictions or restraints. For some insane reason they gave it up—him now in the jewelry business married to a Barbara and her, the equivalent, married to a Thaddeus living in Saint Albans. Both burdened, miserable—joy only a memory.

To get through the rest of the session she registers some obligatory complaints about her husband. Jonathan responds appropriately. They're snapped into roles. When the time is up he doesn't say anything. She knows the time is up also. They simply sit there. She stares at the floor and he stares at some point over her head. Neither wants to leave. His next appointment, a woman who is trying to get her alcoholic husband into a program, is in the waiting room. He usually comes out and gets his next appointment but now he simply sits. He can't envision life without Beverly in his presence.

Beverly has to pick Janelle up from her mother's house in Laurelton. Her mother has a doctor's appointment and will be cross if Beverly is late. Beverly doesn't have a car—they are not a two-car family. She has to catch the bus on Hillside Avenue. It's pretty reliable but she can tell her mother that today it was late. She's not going to leave unless he asks her to. She'll sit there till the cows come home.

There's a rough tap on the door.

"Yes," Jonathan says. "Come in."

Luella Peters, the receptionist, yanks opens the door.

"Mrs. Johnson is here."

"Oh, of course . . . ran a little over . . ."

Beverly and Jonathan stand and face each other—social half-smiles on their faces.

"Till next time then," he says.

"Yes, thank you."

Beverly moves smoothly past the bulk of Mrs. Peters in the doorway. Mrs. Peters sniffs the atmosphere. Something here. She doesn't trust this young white boy. He has a sneaky roving eye. And this Mrs. Carmichael. Uppity. Who the hell does she think she is anyway? She just a poor nigger here in Jamaica Queens trying to get by just like the rest of us, honey.

Sure got some shape though.

Chapter Four

Jonathan watches them file into his office and take their seats. Beverly on the left and Thaddeus on the right. They seem formal, almost stiff. Each cross their legs, Beverly's right to left, Thaddeus's left to right. Jonathan gazes at the space between them, a tentative smile waiting to be hurled out. He's grateful Thaddeus doesn't reach out to shake his hand the way he did when he left after the last session. He's been trained to have as little physical contact as possible with clients because the extra dimension of touch and the chance of smell can add dangerous and unpredictable dimensions to the therapeutic encounter.

Actually that was the only part of the experience with the Carmichaels he'd spoken about with Timothy.

"I have this client at the center who almost knocked me over to shake my hand after his session with me. I didn't know how to discourage it. I didn't like it. His handshake was too strong. He got right up into my face, thanked me, and told me what a wonderful session it was. He's a life insurance salesman."

"What else is he?"

"What do you mean?"

"Is he old, young, tall, short, fat, skinny, black, yellow, good breath, bad breath?"

"Young, medium, black, and Clorets."

"By initially telling me he's a life insurance salesman you're encouraging me to think stereotype. I wonder why that is? I had a gentleman over to sell me life insurance recently and he was quite reserved, soft-spoken, and not pushy at all. Frankly, I'd have preferred someone more outgoing—even pushy. I didn't buy the policy because he didn't do or say anything to get me to buy. I need the insurance so if I happen to die my significant other will be in dire straits because of a shy life insurance man. Just thought I'd share that with you."

"Thank you. I see your point. Maybe I didn't like the control over me this client had."

"Is that all you didn't like?"

"What else do you think?"

"Ha!"

"I know you want me to say something about race."

"How do you know that?"

"Because there is something to say about race and I suppose I'm not saying it or wanting to think about it."

"Go on."

"I've had very little contact, skin to skin, with African Americans. Oh, there's some in school I know by name and they've come over to the house and done work for my family and of course there's the cleaning girl . . ."

"And there you are in the heart of Jamaica, Queens, 99 percent African American, administering to the psychological needs of the population."

"I'm not a bigot." Jonathan would have liked to back that up with his equal opportunity love-lust for Beverly but he wasn't quite set to go there yet . . . perhaps all this might lead to it . . . let it flow naturally and if there's a dam that doesn't allow it to come out this session, well, so be it . . . maybe next session . . . maybe not at all. He'd not allowed himself to masturbate Beverly away—not just yet. He's keeping her in a special place. If he has a crush on her, it'll vanish on its own . . . meanwhile he likes to keep it safe, hidden, and warm. Jerking off on it will make it tacky and mundane, like last month's *Playboy*.

"I didn't accuse you of being a bigot," Timothy says.

"It seems as if you're leading to that."

"Natural avoidance of the unfamiliar is bigotry only when coupled with narrow-mindedness and meanness of spirit. Look, it's like you were brought up to believe all little green apples are bad for you—they're inferior and rotten on the inside so you don't eat them—keep far away from them because maybe even looking at one or touching one would contaminate you. Then they come along and tell you little green apples are okay. They prove it to you by scientific evidence and everyone says yeah go ahead and take a bite and you say sure it's okay but it's only your head talking not your gastric juices, not your taste buds, not all the body chemistry that's been misdirected all these years so you can't. That's not being a bigot or a racist because you know those green apples are as good as sweet peaches and juicy plums but it's the chemistry. Up until recently blacks meant a certain thing, not only to you but to almost everyone with your upbringing. To suddenly pretend because of certain laws and changes going on in society that this part of our human makeup doesn't exist is a form of a wish-fulfillment fantasy you don't want to engage in."

Sometimes, surprisingly, Dr. Timothy Mitchell could be comforting.

"I'd like to bring up something," Beverly says in a determined fashion. She pauses, waiting for Thaddeus to intrude, and then goes on when he doesn't. "My cousin Faith is getting married this weekend. We are going to the church on Saturday afternoon and then a reception afterward at the Regency Catering Hall."

Beverly caresses "Regency" with this island lilt of hers that lets Jonathan know there's an importance to the place. Thaddeus knows what the importance is. He resents the caress because to him it's a warning. The Regency is on the North Shore of Long Island in Dix Hills, a mostly white prosperous neighborhood. The band will be white guys—a mixture of Jewish and Italian—and the caterer also white. This will be one of the Regency's few black catering jobs. The caterer justifies this by letting everyone know they're Jamaicans. "You know the ones that come over here and buy houses right off. They're so clean you can eat off the floor."

"I do not wish to be embarrassed, as I always am, when my family gets together, by my husband making a nuisance of himself attempting to sell everyone he sees a policy."

She doesn't say especially in a situation where the entire crowd of guests will be judged as far as behavior and comportment are concerned. Thaddeus will be one of the few black Americans in the crowd and he will wind up bringing disgrace on all the others. They will think we are all like him.

Thaddeus works the crowd at gatherings of any kind. The guests, the clergy, the band, the caterer, the waiters. There he is up close and personal, touching body parts as he talks, his card out, his pen working, getting phone numbers, rapping about this plan or that while the poor captive only wants to dance and drink. Beverly makes as if she doesn't even know him. She turns him down when he wants to dance with her (only after he's filled his pockets with enough leads to satiate himself).

"A few months ago," Thaddeus explains in an uncharacter-istically calm manner, "we attended a wedding and I spoke to a cousin of hers, Eric Priestly, who had absolutely turned me down when I tried to sell him a policy previously."

Beverly makes a rude little noise and looks out of the grimy window at the scruffy brick wall of the adjacent build-ing. She knows this story all too well. Thaddeus, like a martyr being struck by a rock, blinks not an eye and continues to explain.

"We had a drink or two and then he softened up and signed for a policy right there and then. I always keep an application and a rate card with me . . . you never know. A month and a half later Eric was killed in a car accident. And two weeks after, I delivered a check payable to the widow, Mrs. Blanche Priestly, for the sum of $100,000. A $50,000 policy with an accidental death clause. Eric Priestly had only given me sixty dollars to bind the policy. The policy had not even been issued yet. That $100,000 will make the difference between demeaning, grinding poverty for the widow and her two children and hold your-head-up-high dignity and educa-tion for those two young boys. I have a calling. I spread the word. I can make a difference!"

"You've had this discussion before?" Jonathan asks.

"I cannot discuss it with him," Beverly asserts. "He will not give this up. He doesn't care how embarrassed I am."

"Is that so?" Jonathan asks Thaddeus.

"No, I do care about how embarrassed she is," Thaddeus replies. "But I can't help it. It's what I do. It's what I like to do. Sure, I know I'm viewed as pushy and obnoxious by some people. Blanche Priestly thought I was obnoxious too—until I handed her that check for $100,000 that is."

"Can we come to some middle ground here," Jonathan says. "Some point where there's a significant decrease in embarrassment while there still can be a certain amount of promotion?"

The married couple pause to consider Jonathan's proposal seriously.

"All right, here's what I'll do," Thaddeus says. "I'll just go around and meet the people and then I'll get a list of their names and call them on the phone during the week. What about that?"

Thaddeus gazes at Beverly's profile as she considers.

"That would be better," she says.

They've taken the first step. The process is working. This surprisingly alarms Thaddeus. He thinks about what happened yesterday.

Thaddeus moved into the pocket park behind the Hillside General Office of the Meridian Life Insurance Company. There's a little lake there with ducks, a couple of old swans, surrounded by a playground and park benches. The park was filled on this sunny, early spring day with seniors and mothers with their preschoolers—the only black person was an old park attendant, picking up paper with a metal pointed stick and putting it into a sack. As Thaddeus passed the man they do not acknowledge one another outwardly but inwardly they do. Thaddeus was wearing a dark, double-breasted suit with stripes, carrying an alligator attaché case, shoes bright, very sharp. I ain't going to be like you, Thaddeus thought, passing the park attendant stabbing a Snickers wrapper.

Old man this is the best you could do, he thought—hell not bad really, civil service, get you a pension and all but the only suit you own is your church suit. Your shoulders sag cause you so used to looking on the ground for the white man's crumbs. Not me brother. Not me.

The park attendant viewed a new, young arrogance moving past him and wondered where it will all lead. In a way he felt sad for the young man. You think they going to let you in at last, do you? They makin' a show now cause of politics but it ain't really goin' to happen. You in for a big fall, my arrogant young brother. A big fall.

There were two young white girls eating their lunch on a park bench by the lake. Donna and Maureen. Donna's a dark, Italian girl, almost thirty, working at the Hillside Office for over a year, having an affair with the general manager, Colonel Carrington. She's upset because he's obviously not faithful to her in the same way he's not faithful to his wife with her and her hard-edge morality's cracking because she's beginning to care about him. Maureen has been giving her traditional advice and solace. She ought to break up. He's a married man. But Maureen's been thinking about Thaddeus lately and wondering what a relationship with him would be like so her own advice was beginning to sound hollow to her. And then she blinked and there's Thaddeus walking toward her.

He sat down without being invited, pretending to be surprised he'd run into them this way. Donna would like Maureen to be in the same boat she's in. Why shouldn't this young Irish kid have a go at it too? Hell, there were good times, when it first started. She really liked being with a black married guy giving church and family the finger. She felt real sophisticated. Too bad she's kind of bummed out now with this Colonel thing. Why should she be the only one? She scampered off telling Maureen and Thaddeus she had to do some shopping.

They sat for a while pretending to dig the old swans. Maureen's a large, freckled girl with bright blue eyes and brown hair. There's a sweetness about her that has melted Thaddeus's normal aggressiveness toward women so he's usually on his best behavior around her and now he's uncharacteristically tongue-tied. Then . . . "Can I see you after work sometime?"

Maureen's been expecting this and she's had her answer prepared but now she can't get it out. She's not into any new age morality in particular and had no strong feeling about race. She's gone to school with blacks and doesn't find anything strange about them. She knew there's injustice but hasn't thought much about it. Now that the invitation was posed she felt her nice, little, straight, Catholic girl speech may deprive her of some sort of important experience, something undefined, that might help her grow up. She's been feeling slow compared to some of her friends who have graduated college and were doing more worldly, interesting things than she was, like working for an insurance company, essentially waiting to get married. She viewed her future with a sad kind of equanimity.

She didn't answer. She simply got up and walked around the lake and of course Thaddeus was at her side and they were walking openly. She became aware of covert glances, an umbrella of disapproval that now covered the little park. She's annoyed at that. Hey, come into the twenty-first century you narrow-minded Queens people. People ought to be with whomever. No one was inferior or superior.

Thaddeus wasn't quite sure she'd heard his offer. He didn't know if he ought to ask her again or simply skip it and wait for another time. She's easy to walk with, not ashamed to be seen with him, he surmised, and he could love her just for that. They passed a curly haired, little boy being strolled by his mother and Maureen smiled easily at the mother and child and said, "Cute . . ." The mother smiled a thank you back at Maureen.

There's a copse. Thaddeus noticed it on coming into the park without being fully aware why. He took Maureen's hand

and led her into the green hideaway. He faced her and ran his finger over the freckles on her face. She gazed at his spiky whiskers and wondered if they're as bristly as they looked. Then he kissed her softly on the mouth. She let out a breath and said, "No . . ." and backed away till she's up against a tree. "Please . . ."

Having kissed her he didn't want to stop. He moved to her again and when he kissed her this time she opened her mouth. She felt his hard-on against her leg and then his hand on her breast. His whiskers felt soft and had a pleasant scent. She put her hands on both his shoulders.

"That's enough," she says. "Enough."

He backed off.

"For now?" he asked.

She moved out of the copse and quickly walked back to work.

An agreement. Jonathan feels triumphant. He's a good counselor; able to overcome his own drives to do his job! If he were a really destructive person he would not be able to have these clients take this first important step. This silly little thing he has for Beverly did not really get in the way. This couple can now see the benefits of laying their feelings on the table and working out rational agreements. He's really proud of himself.

Maybe he'll jerk off later.

He beams at his clients.

Beverly's been forced to enter a reasonable process. Is this what the rest of her life will be like? Reasonable but miserable with this buffoon!? Yet she admires Jonathan for getting Thaddeus to change. Thank God she's not going to be embarrassed at the wedding! She wonders if Jonathan has a good sense of humor like Sheldon.

"I heard that Jamaican girls are the JAPs of the Caribbean," Sheldon told her when they first met. He was playing drums at a club in the Village. He came to the table during a break because he knew her date, James Tarrington, who had a steel drum band. She'd been glad because she couldn't take her eyes off him with his wild hair and big toothy grin.

"What does that mean?" she'd asked.

"Jewish American Princess. Jamaican American Princess. Same acronym. Frigid, mercenary, tough, and cold."

She was being teased and liked it. Is Jonathan teasing her now by making her come to an agreement with Thaddeus? Is he really playing at this counselor thing?

Thaddeus is justifying his pushiness by telling Jonathan how much he wants to make a lot of money so his daughter can have the best things in life.

"Look at that body language!" Thaddeus suddenly turning on Beverly. "I'm pouring my heart out about our daughter's future and she acting as if she's sitting through a bad movie."

She's been slumping and glancing at her watch. A Piaget, gotten for her by Thaddeus in the good old days with American Express.

"A bad movie at least is going to end at some point," she says. "He spends money like water. Seven-hundred-dollar suits. Best ties and shirts . . . shoes. Drives a Mercedes he can hardly pay for. Where is the concern for our daughter's future there?"

"I need to keep up appearances for my business. No one wants to deal with a man who doesn't ooze success out of every pore."

"What about your damn underwear. Won't catch you with no Hanes. Shops in SoHo for pastel colors with a bikini cut. I wonder who you're oozing success for there."

"Do you see what she's implying?" Thaddeus states righteously.

"I think we ought to consider what's just happened here," Jonathan says. "We start out by coming to a very amicable agreement regarding a situation that has, in the past, caused a great deal of friction. One would think that would lead the way to further agreements, but it seems as if the opposite's occurred. Both of you now become solidly entrenched in bitterness and anger. Do you feel, and I'm just throwing this out here for consideration—I may be all wrong—but do you feel there's any connection?"

"Connection?" Thaddeus asks. "How?"

"Between coming to an agreement," Beverly explains to Thaddeus as if he's slightly retarded, "and then starting to fight."

"Oh? Like . . . ?"

"Like the smart man is saying," Beverly interprets. "Maybe we really don't want to agree."

"Then why are we here?" Thaddeus asks to no one in particular, actually puzzled.

"Yes." Jonathan looks at one and then the other. "Why are you here?"

There's a deafening silence.

"Janelle," Thaddeus says.

"Yes," Beverly reluctantly agrees. "Janelle."

Jonathan waits.

"That's not really a good reason, is it?" Beverly says.

Jonathan looks to Thaddeus.

"It should be more than that, shouldn't it?" Thaddeus says.

"Maybe there is," Jonathan says. "And we just need to discover it."

No, that's not what Beverly thinks. This is the old Freudian gobbledygook. Sheldon would do that shit all the time. Jewish boys are good at it, like Catholic priests, turning everything that goes on in the world into expressions of faith in God. The Catholic priest will have his hand up the altar boy's leg even as he's preaching and the Jewish boy will have his hand up your skirt as he's twisting Freud like taffy. They love it when you let them know you think they're brilliant so Beverly puts her hand up to her chin as if steeped in sudden awareness.

They go on to talk about Janelle. Thaddeus spoils the child, according to Beverly, while Beverly is far too stern, according to Thaddeus. Thaddeus openly disagrees with Beverly's discipline. Just last evening there was a fight because Beverly tried to take the TV away from Janelle because she was watching too much and Thaddeus insisted she could watch—all this in front of Janelle who cried pitiably so her father would even be more on her side.

Jonathan goes into the ramifications of parents fighting in front of their children and the harm it does the child. Even if they do disagree they ought to do so privately and then come to a standard operating agreement that will not conflict the child.

Thaddeus is again inclined to be reasonable. He concedes he will allow Beverly slack when it comes to discipline and not interfere. Thaddeus notices the more he concedes the puffier Jewboy gets, looking more and more like a hero in Bitch Beverly's eyes.

Thaddeus kind of enjoys being a reasonable guy. Maybe he's rehearsing for his future life with Maureen—making himself worthy of her by ironing out kinks in his personality.

Maybe he has been a real son of a bitch for a woman to live with. Ought to be grateful he's had a run-through with Beverly before he gets to the real thing with Maureen. Beverly's like spring training. Maureen, the season.

Jonathan's split. Glorying, on one hand, at the great job he's doing, rewarded by Beverly's obvious appreciation, yet troubled by a certain hollowness to the entire procedure. Beverly doesn't seem to react very positively to Thaddeus's concessions and Thaddeus is giving ground as if it's infested with crocodiles in the swampland he used to sell in Florida. Jonathan's fascinated at this phenomenon and somewhat impatient to get to individual sessions with these engrossing (for different reasons) people so he can get to the bottom of the mystery.

The session proceeds to its conclusion. Issues defined for the future. Textbook session except everything seems artificial.

Time's up. Jonathan calls a halt and rises. He doesn't want to shake hands with Thaddeus so he sticks a yellow pad in one hand and a pen in the other as he goes to the door to open it and let them out. Beverly almost brushes his chest. Thaddeus notices a bit of an undulation in Beverly's walk.

Luella Peters notices the threesome coming out of the office. All acting a bit strange, like a group of guys shooting craps when they ought to be working. She wonders what the hell is going on.

꙳

Maureen tells Thaddeus when he calls her on the interoffice phone and asks to see her after work that she will meet him during her lunch hour and maybe take a ride in his car to talk things over.

She's not really sure why she's doing this. She's attracted but knows she won't do anything about the attraction. She has a few guys she sees on an intermittent basis—nice guys ranging from twenty-two to twenty-nine. She's not in love at this moment though she sleeps with each of them from time to time if the circumstances are okay. She's quite comfortable with sleeping with a guy without having to be in love. When she was first in love, at nineteen, with this Armenian boy Gregory she was terribly hurt when he proved two-faced and started to go with another girl. Maybe she's getting a bit hard-edged about guys at twenty-two, not easily prone to giving her emotions away and she doesn't like that about herself. She always has to be a little drunk to have sex and sometimes in the middle of it she asks herself what the hell she's doing. Then she'll remember making love those first few times with Gregory and she'll often stifle tears and shut her mind down to go on with it.

She almost wishes she had the same racial attitudes as almost everyone else. Is there something wrong with her to not be as deeply pissed off as her family with all this affirmative action stuff? Maureen doesn't argue with them but she basically feels blacks have been treated so badly all these years it's about time they got a break. She always kind of liked black guys. She loves Will Smith and would like to hang his picture on her bedroom wall but she's too afraid.

She tells Thaddeus she'll be walking down 168th Street toward Jamaica Avenue at 12:35 and if he happens to be passing by and stops she'll get in his car, which is exactly what happens. Once she's safely inside, Thaddeus guns the car as quickly as he can so as not to be seen by anyone in the office. He makes a right on Jamaica Avenue and without even realizing it he passes by the office building where he goes for marriage counseling.

"What's the matter?" Maureen asks him. They'd been silent, feeling how it is to be alone together now on a prearranged occasion.

"I just drove past where I go for marriage counseling."

"I guess you need it," Maureen chuckles.

"I guess so."

Thaddeus has scouted out a little street in Ozone Park, near a ball field, where he can park and be fairly private in the middle of the afternoon. When he parks, turns off the engine, faces Maureen, and moves to kiss her, she puts her hand on his shoulder and gently pushes him back.

"Let's talk," she says.

"Sure."

"I don't fool around with married guys," she says, watching him carefully.

"So what am I supposed to do now?"

"I just wanted to let you know."

"Yeah, okay, no matter what, right? No matter what else is going on between the married guy and you, right?"

"There's no future for a girl with a married man."

"There don't have to be a future, only a present. This future business you know it fucks us all up if you'll pardon the French. You ain't supposed to live because of something or something about your future. You know what, the future was a minute ago and when I tried to kiss you now it's the past and you ain't experienced the pleasure of the kiss. Your future could have been kissing me—right now which is really what you want to do instead you making with this yad-da-da-yad-da-da-yad-da-da stuff about married men and shit. Come on, girl, I kissed you before and that was the sweetest kiss I ever had in my whole life and you know what I felt? I felt it was the same for you too but I also felt you'd make yourself not think about it because you were too afraid of where your feelings were going to take you, right?"

Thaddeus is up close prodding her arm and shoulders as he talks. She doesn't want to face him because she's about to cry. He's right. She didn't think about how she felt when they kissed. She's been miserable and unable to sleep since it happened. She turns to Thaddeus and looks at him full face. Guy's not really Will Smith cute but she wants to run her hand through those whiskers again and so before she knows what she's doing she's stroking his face and then they're kissing. Her arms snake around his neck. He lays her down on the seat and she feels his hard-on moving aggressively on her leg and she moves into it, getting wet, wishing his hands, now all over her breasts, would move down between her legs and stroke her thighs. And then she wants to feel his finger in her vagina, wants to fuck him here and now, but she's suddenly afraid of getting caught in broad daylight with a black guy. The cops will think she's a hooker. She sits up and gets Thaddeus off her.

"Not here," she mumbles.

"Okay. Where?"

"I don't know why I'm doing this. What's the matter with me? I do want you but it's not right. I wish I could go to a priest so's I can be talked out of it. Maybe a girlfriend or something . . . but only these days no one's there except your mom to tell you it's not right. Listen, you're a married guy with problems, right? How does you having anything to do with me help you?"

"I don't know. I don't care."

"Okay, it's none of my business. I'm not getting involved with you that way, am I?"

"No, none of that."

"You just want to have some fun."

"Right."

"Well, maybe so do I. That's the new thing. Girls just want to have fun."

"Damn right."

She reaches down and feels his still hard penis and they kiss again. She jams her tongue into his mouth and unzips him just when a car pulls into the driveway next door and a big white guy steps out. Thaddeus backs the car out and drives away.

"I can't wait to see you naked," he tells her. "Be in bed with you."

"I wasn't going to fool around with you. I was going to tell you no. Now I couldn't stop if I wanted to. Listen, one thing, don't hurt me. I know you're married and stuff and that's all right. Don't try to get me emotional. We'll fool around and then like go on our way. I don't want to interfere in your marriage or even hear about it."

"Yeah, okay."

"Let's get back to the office now. My lunch time is almost up."

They drive toward the office, his hand all the way up her dress and hers on his still erect cock. Thaddeus pulls in front of the office building where he goes for marriage counseling and parks at a meter that has time on it. He gets from behind the wheel, drops to his knees, spreads her legs, burrows between her thighs, pulls her panties off, and puts the tip of his tongue right up on her clitoris. She giggles to cover up the rush. She moves her cunt into him. She doesn't at all think about where she is, people passing in front of her on their way shopping or to their offices. No one noticing her as she sits, eyes wide open with Thaddeus kneeling on the floor, tongue probing inside her.

Then they switch places. He sits up and Maureen gets on her knees. She wants to taste him. Thaddeus leans back and idly gazes at the window in a hazy state of ecstasy. He lazily watches as someone slows down and stares into the car. It's a guy with big round eyes that look vaguely familiar. The guy moves to the car and Thaddeus has an idea that he ought to tell Maureen to get off her knees because this guy might be a cop or something but everything is so slow motion in a fast way that all he can do is stare up at this guy and wait for him to go but instead the guy's at the window trying to say something to him and all at once Thaddeus realizes it's Jonathan Meltzer, his marriage counselor, who is there simply trying to say hello, at least until he notices Maureen on her knees with Thaddeus's dick in her mouth. Maureen then feels Thaddeus tighten and she looks up and to her left and there's this guy with eyes popping. For a moment she thinks it might be her older brother Sean, who is a detective, and she panics. She bites down and Thaddeus winces in pain. But then she lets up and simply plops on the floor.

Jonathan, his friendly hello frozen on his face, whirls around and hurriedly moves down the street.

Thaddeus helps Maureen up off the floor. They arrange themselves and he drives back to the office.

"Who was that?" she asks.

"Our marriage counselor."

❧

"I think I need to come clean," Jonathan tells Dr. Timothy. "I've been holding back. I've been in the midst of a kind of . . . well not dilemma because I'm not confronted with any clear choices but a situation that has brought me some moral anguish."

"Moral anguish?" Timothy says. "What theater review did you get that phrase from? What does it mean? Why don't you simply tell me what is going on."

"Well, I'm treating this couple . . ."

"Yeah, the black guy who confuses you . . ."

"I treat a lot of African Americans . . ."

"But you've only spoken about one. The life insurance salesman—the one with a wife . . ."

"I never talked about the wife."

"Exactly."

"What are you telling me?"

"I'm telling you sometimes you can say more without saying anything. Sometimes it's what you leave out that counts more than what you leave in."

"You're only telling me you're smart. You're blowing your own horn instead of letting me give you the material."

"You're right. Okay, I'm an egocentric, sophomoric practitioner so anything liable to come out concerning your 'moral anguish' will not be really valid, will it?"

"I'm so fucking upset I don't even know why. It's everything!"

"Go on."

"Okay, I'm treating this couple and I'm starting to . . . get the rocks for this woman."

"The rocks? What does 'the rocks' mean?"

"Means I'm becoming attracted to her—sexually. No, it doesn't mean just that. If it was just that maybe I'd have the kind of problem I could masturbate away. I can't even jerk off thinking about her. I . . . think . . . it sounds crazy . . . I almost feel like telling you not to laugh but I think I'm in love with her."

"Why do you think it's love?"

"Because that's what I keep thinking. I think about her all the time . . . not just in a sexual way though . . . I see her face and the way she moves and the lilt in her voice and the way her cheeks curve on her face. I imagine us together in nice ways . . . walking and talking and eating dinner. When she smiles, which hasn't been very often, but when she does her face radiates and it is the most beautiful face I have ever seen. I imagine her with a little baby in her arms, our baby, breast-feeding and changing her diaper—it's a girl . . . I've imagined it to be a girl . . . the most beautiful girl you'd ever hope to see. A mixed kid. Beverly, her name is Beverly . . . is a light-skinned Jamaican woman and I imagine our kid would be one of those sensational mixed kids with a combination blue-green eyes and tawny skin, curly hair—I love beautiful mixed kids. I go on and on about her in my head. Detail after detail. Yet I know I'm crazy. Not only is she my client along with her husband . . . more on that . . . but she's really got enormous hang-ups. She's like a gold digger. What am I trying to do, ruin my life?! Help me get over it. It's a disaster!"

"Do you want to get over it?"

"Of course."

"What do you mean of course?"

"It's wrong."

"Tell me what's wrong about it?"

"You are some therapist. If I came in here and talked about murdering someone, you'd ask well what's wrong with it."

"You're talking about loving somebody not murdering them."

That stops Jonathan. He pauses. Breathing fast, almost dizzy. "You mean it's not a bad thing?" he manages to say.

"You're emotional now. You've always been very unemotional. I deal in emotions. I welcome it. Don't worry right or wrong. Let it out, *boychik*, let it out."

"There's more. There's what brought this entire thing to such an aggravating head . . . oh god . . . talking about head . . ."

"Go on, talk about head . . ."

"I'm walking to lunch today. I make a left turn out of my building to the little luncheonette on the corner. I'm going to start my first day of a diet. I want to lose weight ever since I've been obsessing about Beverly. I'm going to order a simple tuna on dry toast and coffee. No butter. No ice cream for dessert. I'm going to drop fifteen pounds, really get serious about tennis . . . the whole thing. There's a car parked right outside my building and who is in it but Beverly's husband, the life insurance guy . . . he's seated in the passenger seat . . . I smile at him and walk over. I'm glad to see him."

"Why?"

"Because I think I'll see Beverly too. She may be in a store or something and if I linger for a few words with the guy . . ."

"Whose name is?"

"Thaddeus . . . if I shoot the shit just a little bit I'll see her on the street and maybe she'll look different in other surroundings and I can start to forget her. That's why I'm glad to see Thaddeus. So I walk over to the car but I notice his eyes widen and a look of apprehension crosses his face. And then, through the window, as I approach the car, I see a woman on her knees in front of him. His pants are down. My heart sinks. It's her. Beverly. They're not supposed to be getting along and there she is—my God giving him a blow job in the middle of the afternoon right outside my office. A severe stab of indignation and jealousy cuts through me like a knife. Are they putting me on? Testing me? Then the woman looks up at me and it isn't Beverly. It's like this . . . white girl . . . I figure maybe a hooker or something except she kind of looks respectable . . . at least without Thaddeus's dick in her mouth. I scamper the hell out of that scene. When I turn around they're off. I go into the diner and order a jumbo hamburger with french fries and mayo. Ice cream for dessert too."

"How do you feel in the diner?"

"Shocked but then—confused."

"Your entire psyche is exposed through this encounter. It's almost too good to be true. It's like an enormously lucid dream. I'm rolling up my sleeves."

"I'm incredibly pissed off at this Thaddeus. It's as if he's been put on earth to bedevil every hang-up I own—large and small, he pricks them, if you'll pardon the use of that word. I never thought like this before—like me being in charge. Me being in AUTHORITY though strictly speaking a marriage counselor is not an authority figure."

"So how do you feel about this guy? Edit nothing."

"How dare that fucking . . ."

"Say it."

"How dare that fucking . . . guy . . ."

"No!!! Say it, damn it."

"Let me express it my way."

"Your way is what you feel like saying. Say it, you fucking fat ass Jewboy!!!"

"Is that what you think of me?!!!"

"Sometimes! Yes. Sometimes I do! Now what do you think of this Thaddeus? How dare that fucking . . . fucking what . . . ?"

"All right, you cocksucker . . . you far-out Indian fucking, weird excuse for a therapist, I'll say it. How dare that fucking nigger defy my authority by having this little floozy blowing him in the car right outside my office!!"

"Ahh, didn't that feel good?"

"No, it's horrible. I've never said that word before."

"What word? Fucking?"

"Want me to say it again? Make you happy?"

"Yes. Very fucking happy."

"Nigger! Nigger! Dirty, no good, cotton-picking, low-life nigger!!! Okay? Now you say what you think about me."

"Jewboy! Kike! Hebe! Christ killer! How's that?"

"So what the fuck are we proving?"

"Think about it."

"I can't think about anything," Jonathan tells Timothy. "I'm so angry at you for what you called me."

"Why?"

"It shows me how you really feel about me. I don't know if I can continue with you now."

"Why?"

"I hate bigotry."

"I hate bigotry too."

"You were only role-playing, weren't you?" Jonathan asks.

"No, I was being totally honest with you."

"I'm going to leave now . . . before the session is over. Very unJew like . . . paying for the whole session and not using it. Right?"

Thaddeus is dead on time. He's normally a few minutes late. He's developed a nice rapport with Luella Peters. He's been telling her about the benefits of a good retirement plan and she's promised to go home and talk to her husband about it but she hasn't because she's simply playing Thaddeus along, basking in being paid attention to by this sharp dude with the knockout, snooty wife. She wouldn't mind tipping with someone like him but she knows her days of being able to attract a young buck are far behind her. Still, she could show him a good time if he'd let her.

Jonathan, his eyes fixed on his wristwatch, becomes anxious. He knows Thaddeus is there because he sneaked a look. Now he interrupts the intense conversation between Mrs. Peters and Thaddeus. Thaddeus smiles at him, grabs his arm, flashes a toothy smile, and says, "Hey, how you doin' man?"

"Fine," Jonathan says dryly.

They face each other, seated, and Thaddeus emits a man-to-man grin. Hey, listen, the grin says, we guys know the real truth about ourselves. The damn women can run their motherfucking mouths about all that other shit but we know we want all the pussy we can get. A man has to maintain some family structure and shit but his real heart and soul lies in the pussy he can sneak. Now what are you going to tell me about what you seen yesterday? Why can't you throw your arm around my shoulder in a sign of universal brotherhood and say hey man maybe you fix me up too. Come on Mr. Jonathan Future Doctor Meltzer, be who you really are!

Jonathan doesn't crack his lips. No comradeship grin from him. He glares. "Can I ask you something?" Jonathan mutters through tight lips.

"Sure, ask away." Thaddeus magnanimous, expansive.

"Why in front of my building?"

"Just the same question she asked."

"Who?"

"Maureen, the girl from my office, who you sort of met yesterday. I thought she'd be pissed at being spotted like that but she thought it was kind of funny. She is something else that girl—like liberated and shit. What'd you think of her? I mean you didn't get a full view but she is foxy man. And you know what? No one has ever given me head like that before in my whole motherfucking life. And you know what? I had me a breakthrough. You going to be glad about this because I think I went a long way in overcoming my female problem—you know, not being real sensitive to bitches and all. I went down on her. I just went down and ate her motherfucking pussy like it was chitterlings. I never ate no pussy before. Never. It was a breakthrough man!"

"I suppose you want me to be happy about your 'breakthrough'?" Jonathan asks Thaddeus, unable to keep an angry edge from his voice. When Thaddeus doesn't answer, Jonathan says, "You come to me to help you save your marriage. You have a child—two years old—who you profess to love."

"I do love her, man," Thaddeus snaps.

"Then you need to bring her up in a sound family structure. I want to help you. I'm trained and committed to help you. I became a therapist because I care deeply about helping people. I sincerely think if you iron out your difficulties you can be happy. We have to consider what you did. I'm not talking simply about infidelity. We all know it occurs even in relatively stable marriages. But you expressed something when you arranged that scene in front of my office building. It's going to be important for us to work out what you were expressing."

"You know what I was expressing?"

"Go on."

"I was expressing having a hard-on for this girl right there. I saw a parking space with time on the meter so I wouldn't have to get out of the car with my motherfucking pants bulging all over the place. I didn't even think about where that parking space was."

"Is that the only level you're going to consider?"

"Are you saying I lack the depth to consider other levels?" Thaddeus asks in a challenging way.

"No, I'm not saying that."

"Are you saying I'm dumb?"

"No. I'm asking what is it you want me to do now? You are the client."

"Do what you been doing. What's the big deal?"

Thaddeus has Jonathan all tied up in knots. Everything in him cries out against treating someone in a marriage that is blatantly unfaithful. Yet, his training tells him to be non-judgmental—all situations do not conform to the American pattern of fidelity that Europeans laugh at so much. Nothing perfect in this world, his mother always says, though she's always really thought of herself as having no imperfection.

This client's wishes are for a stable married life with a girl-friend or two on the side. Okay, who is he, Jonathan Meltzer, to make an adverse judgment? By this time he has thought about the lesson inflicted on him by Timothy and he's decided to call for another appointment. We all have our prejudices, Jonathan concluded, though being called those disgusting names still rankles. So he has to reconcile his own bigotry, part of which is accepting Thaddeus Carmichael's goals for therapy. He can do that or he can refuse to treat this marriage and get the head of the clinic, Dr. Leonard Warren, to assign this case to someone else. Except . . . he wouldn't see Beverly anymore . . .

"Besides," Thaddeus says, "she do the same thing."

"What?"

"My wife do the same thing."

"You know that?"

"Absolutely."

"For sure?"

"Well, I ain't caught no dude between her legs but I know she do. She has to."

"Has to?"

"Man, that bitch so hot she got to or she burst into flame from keeping all that heat inside. Got jungle fever in her pussy. She ain't giving me shit so it's got to go somewhere . . . dig? We got people comin' to the house all the time—delivery*men,* post*men,* home improvement sales*men,* even life insurance sales*men.* She do anyone take her fancy." You too white boy, Thaddeus thinks as he watches Jonathan attempt to stifle the image of all that jungle fever in Beverly's pussy. "Woman's cli-toris like a beanstalk—go up to the sky every time a Jack come near it."

"If you think that . . . ?" Jonathan stammers.

"I don't think it, I know it. Birds got to fly, fish got to swim. Beverly's got to have it. Steady."

"How does that make you feel?" Jonathan asks.

"I suppose what's good for the gander is good for the goose," Thaddeus says. "I used to be a little upset about it. You know come home at unexpected times see if I can catch some motherfucka but she too smart for that. She always dropping Janelle off at her mother's and then getting these guys to take her to a fine hotel—she don't like motels. She must know every hotel in the city by this time. Shit, that's why she got this degree in hotel management. Before we married even though I had my own pad bitch made me take her to a fancy hotel most of the time—right there at the desk with me—no shame when I signed for the room. Told me I didn't have to put down no Mr. and Mrs. That's bullshit. You put down my name. I don't do anything I'm ashamed of. Right there. Then through the lobby and up the elevator bitch'd be critiquing the hotel. See how the hotel clerk was wearing yesterday's shirt with a frayed collar? Lookit that damn rubber plant need trimming. Bitch love hotel beds though. Got her a 'whore complex.' You study that in Freud?"

He's lying. Jonathan knows he's lying. Beverly's not a whore. Jonathan has never wanted to hit anyone but he now has an impulse to reach over his desk and slap Thaddeus Carmichael's mouth shut.

"During the time your wife was suggesting your late hours had very little to do with selling insurance, why didn't you bring these very strong suspicions up?" Jonathan asks.

"Cause I don't want her to know I know."

"Why is that?"

"Because . . . I really love her."

"Um-huh."

"I know that sounds strange to you and it did to me too when I first realized it." Thaddeus is almost mumbling, "I love that woman so much I want her to be happy. I know I don't make her happy—I never really will but I can't let loose of her even if she tears me to shreds. I don't want her to fall in love and leave me and if this little tipping helps her . . ."

"Tipping?"

"That's what colored folks call ladies fooling around . . ."

"Oh . . ."

"If this makes her happy, that's the way it has to be that's all. And besides all that there's another reason. Maybe the real reason."

"What's that?"

"If we break up I lose my daughter."

For the rest of the session Thaddeus complains about the life insurance business, acknowledging a deep ambivalence because selling reinforces a part of his personality he doesn't particularly care for. Some years ago he'd developed a real interest in landscape architecture and had taken courses toward a degree but he dropped out because making money quickly was more important. Now he would like to go back to it but he's beginning to feel hopeless because there'd be years of very little earning and Bitch Beverly'd never stand for it. Yet he realizes he's blaming her for his own lack of courage in never really pursuing his true ambition.

Jonathan listens to all this now only professionally, pondering what he's been told about Beverly's supposed promiscuity. He doesn't believe Thaddeus. Could it be that Thaddeus has discerned how Jonathan feels about Beverly and is talking about her in a way calculated to provoke a certain reaction? Well, what kind of reaction is he actually provoking? Anger and indignation of course, but there's something else Jonathan catches sneaking its ugly head up into the attic of his libido. The image of an easy fuck.

Thaddeus is trying to turn me on to his wife! It's been happening from the very beginning.

But why?

Chapter Five

"I've hardly been able to wait for this session," Beverly tells a trying-to-seem relaxed but immensely tense Jonathan. "I'm awash in self-discovery and self-exploration. I passed by a store just now and in the window was this really cute little bikini and I immediately glanced at my watch to see if I had time to go in and price it and then figure out a way to buy it but then I thought about this watch, a Piaget, way too expensive, that I made Thaddeus buy for me and I thought to myself, why do I need to buy that bikini now? I have many cute bikinis and we really can't afford it. What does that purchase mean to me? And then I thought of my father back in Jamaica—fixing up some furniture for one of the store owners in Kingston—a Jewish man by the name of Schine. I don't know what that means . . . why I thought of it and why I thought it had significance but then I was grateful I was having this session with you because I knew you'd help explore my motivation."

"Did you go into the store?"

"No, no I didn't, though I had time. I knew if I went into the store and acted on my impulse I would lose the insight I might gain by talking about it."

"That's the right thing to do. Now I want you to simply free associate to your image of your father and the Jewish store owner in Kingston."

"All right. Mr. Schine was a very big man. He smoked a big cigar and he drove a big Cadillac car. He liked my father because my father did good work but the thing I remember the most was that my father respected Mr. Schine and spoke about him more highly than I ever heard him speak about anyone."

"In what way did he speak about him?"

"He spoke about Mr. Schine's house, his car, the jewelry his wife and daughter wore—their clothes. I can see him telling my mother, who would listen as if she was in church, about the expensive wallpaper and the antique furniture in the house. They worshipped Mr. Schine."

"Did they worship the man or his possessions?"

"No, the possessions. I'm not even sure if I ever heard them talk about Mr. Schine as a man at all—whether he was kind to his employees or family or did he have a good education or anything. I never thought of him that way either. Whenever he appeared at my father's shop, which was right down the street from our house, the whole neighborhood would perk up and everyone made sure to walk past the store to look at whatever car was parked there and see the big man talking to my father and when that happened my father was the big man—not only in the neighbors' eyes but mine and even my mother would be more respectful to him—for a while anyway. Mr. Schine brought with him a kind of golden glow."

Beverly's also aglow because of the insight gained through her associations. She recalls the scenes vividly, the feel of the grass at home on her bare feet, the jubilation in the neighborhood when Mr. Schine came to her father's shop.

Jonathan can think of a dozen further probes and he will but for the briefest moment he simply pauses to observe her radiance. She gazes at him and suddenly knows how he feels about her. She looks down now, frightened but flushed and pleased—as if Mr. Schine had stopped in the middle of the street before he moved into his big Cadillac and smiled at her, indicating she was a special child, one he would favor in some magical, mysterious way. She remembered then that he had done that once—about to get in the car, looked at her and asked her father if that little girl was his and when her father said yes, "That's my daughter Beverly," Mr. Schine had patted her father on the shoulder and said, "Cute . . . cute little girl . . ." Her father had beamed and she'd felt warm and proud of her six-year-old self.

"I wish you would tell me more about your life in Jamaica," Jonathan says.

"Do you really want to know?"

"Of course."

"Thaddeus never cares to hear about it. Grass huts and bare feet he says. It wasn't that way at all."

She talks about growing up in Jamaica, being very happy there, not at all feeling poor, though her parents tell her they were. She felt poor only when the family came to New York and they needed to buy winter coats and live with a relative in a small brownstone in Brooklyn before they could afford a house in Queens. She's always felt vulnerable in New York, whereas in Jamaica, whenever she's gone back to visit, she's always felt nothing there could harm her. She often thinks she ought to go back, raise her child and leave Thaddeus. However rationally she feels there is really so much more opportunity in America than in Jamaica.

Jonathan can't help thinking of her there—last year he'd gone to Negril with Sheila and toured in a left-side driving car. Being in Negril with Beverly, getting breakfast from the Rastas on the beach, smoking ganja, going back to their room and making love, endlessly high, endlessly turned on.

He feels as if he's on a date with her, getting to know her, and they're sipping a cocktail at a quiet bar before going out to dinner.

"Can I say whatever comes to my mind?" Beverly asks.

"Yes, of course . . ."

"I . . . I'm finding it very difficult to be here with you."

Jonathan holds his breath. Beverly is looking down; it seems as if she's about to cry.

"Why?" Jonathan manages to ask.

"You're too much like a man I was in love with . . ."

"Oh?"

"Sheldon Goldblatt."

Beverly breaks down in a flood of tears. Her shoulders shake. Jonathan stifles a desire to come around his desk to comfort her. Sheldon Goldblatt? A yid like him? She has a thing for Jewish guys? Or maybe she has a thing for all guys, according to Thaddeus.

"We wanted to get married but his parents interfered," Beverly says through tears. "I never realized the force of bigotry in America till that happened to me. They made him stop seeing me. I would have converted to a Jew if they wanted but it really wasn't that. It was because I'm black. Do you think that's fair? Do you think that's right?"

"No, no, of course not."

"Would you let your parents talk you out of marrying the woman you loved because she was black?"

Jonathan shakes his head no but can't say no because not all of him can lie at the same time. He could never, never in one million years come home to his family with a "schvatza." To them it's bad enough he's down here in Jamaica. He heard his mother tell his father it could be dangerous because "who knows who he'll meet down there working amongst them and all that . . . these days anything goes."

"I cannot identify with the black American experience," Beverly goes on. "My people were not slaves. We come to this country for a better life prepared to give to the country as good as we get if not better. We are educated, industrious, and honest but we are lumped with 'them' simply because we are black."

"You've gone through a very hard time," Jonathan says as sympathetically as he can.

"Yes, I would like to forget it . . . put it all behind me and mostly I do except . . . I'm sorry . . . now that I've met you . . ."

The term "met" Jonathan thinks is a distortion. You don't "meet" a therapist, as you "meet" someone at a party or bar. "Meet" is social, it can lead to a date that can lead to a romance that can lead to . . . You don't "meet" a doctor, you go to a doctor . . . say a gynecologist—oh damn, why think of that particular medical specialty?

"Do you still consider yourself in love with Sheldon?" Jonathan asks.

"No, I don't think so. Are you going to ask me if I love my husband?"

"I . . . I wasn't going to but . . ."

"I have no idea why I married him."

"Let's think about it."

"All right, I believe I was playing the role that Sheldon's parents had assigned to me. A no-good black girl getting pregnant out of wedlock. I remember when it happened thinking that hey . . . maybe I could even go on welfare. I walked by the welfare office, even walked in, and the stark reality hit me and I walked back out again. I told my mother about being pregnant—it's not such a terrible thing in our culture. I could live at home and find work and raise my child without a husband but then Thaddeus started hounding me to marry him and I finally gave in because in some way I wanted to be well . . . American respectable. But also I could then show Sheldon's parents that I was really respectable. A husband and a child. Husband an insurance executive—suit and tie . . . not some lazy wino janitor. I'd buy a house on Long Island where they lived and they'd somehow know and see that their son had passed up on a wonderful wife and mother. Crazy, right?"

"No, not at all. Quite often people live out roles they perceive others have assigned them in life."

"I thought I'd forgotten all about Sheldon until I saw you and it all came back in a very painful way."

"How do I remind you of him?"

"You're about the same age and you're Jewish . . . you are Jewish, aren't you . . . that's about all really. You are sensible and sincere—your feet firmly planted on the ground. Sheldon was wild and fun loving and I was always trying to get him to be more . . . well, sensible."

There it is, the sensible and sincere guy that the really knockout girls never go for. The guarded Jonathan as opposed to wild fun-loving Sheldon. The momma's boy. The stick in the mud. The nerd.

"I'm sorry if I've made you feel uncomfortable," Beverly says. "I mean talking about you so personally."

"No, you're supposed to say what comes to mind. You're supposed to react to your therapist. Look at all the important things that have come out."

"Are they important? How will they help me through this jam? I still don't know what to do. To divorce Thaddeus or stay with him?"

"There might be more vital issues at stake."

"What do you mean?"

"The issue of yourself as a person. The problems you yourself have pointed out that you didn't confront until you sought help."

"You mean it really makes little difference what my present situation is unless I make changes within myself? Is that what you mean?"

"Yes."

"But how can I change if I'm still married to him?"

"You've changed already. You told me about your self-awareness with the credit card situation—you were able to stop yourself before you acted out. Beverly, you have an enormous capacity for insight and enlightenment. This experience could be just the beginning for you to open up entirely new paths in the life of your mind as well as the practical life you'll lead from here on in. Let it happen. Go with it. The answer to your current dilemma will become apparent as you go along in possibly surprising and circuitous ways."

Jonathan doesn't feel the need to define circuitous so he feels as if he's making progress with the patronizing side of his bigotry. Mostly he's enjoying the limpid pools of melting acceptance in her eyes as they meet his. They stare at each other. Beverly knows exactly what Jonathan is going through and how he really feels about her, which makes her all at once happy yet sad for him because of his dilemma. She knows he can't and won't do a thing under these circumstances just as she knows that if he did choose to cross the line she would be totally receptive and enormously grateful to take him as a lover.

"Isn't our time up?" she asks suddenly.

They've gone over five minutes. She doesn't want that officious Luella Peters to intrude.

"Yes, I'm afraid it is," he allows himself to say.

She rises. "Thank you," she says, glancing at him briefly.

"Thank you," he replies, stiffly. He doesn't look at her.

"Till next time then," she says. She moves to the door and walks out. When she gets to the hallway just before the elevator she feels like crying.

Jonathan doesn't move as Luella ushers his next client in.

❧

They've made a date to meet after work. When Thaddeus calls Maureen to confirm she tells him she's changed her mind. She tells him she never should have started anything with a married guy. She doesn't want to get hurt. They're better off stopping before they even start. She's stubborn about it—her Irish up when Thaddeus tries to fast-talk her. He becomes nasty. She hangs up on him. Pissed. Justified in refusing him because it's obvious he's insensitive and only really interested in one thing. Of course, supposedly, she's only interested in one thing too but she's afraid it's going to be more if she's not careful. She makes a date with a couple of girlfriends to hang out.

Thaddeus lurks for Maureen in the parking lot of the office building. When she is about to get into her little Honda he pulls his silver Mercedes up to her, sticks his head out, and asks her to follow him. She shakes her head no, gets in the car, and drives away. He pursues.

Maureen lives in Rosedale in a neighborhood peppered with newly moved-in black families. She's angry with Thaddeus for trailing her. He's married, goddamn it. Still she led him on, had that session with him, which she shouldn't have really done. She ought to have known the consequences. She really doesn't want to get involved with a married guy! Why the hell is he still following her in that stupid Mercedes?

Thaddeus doesn't care where this car chase shit is going to end. That girl can't do that kind of shit one minute and then tell him she's through the next. Driving him fucking crazy!

Maureen pulls up under a large tree and parks. Thaddeus pulls up behind her and moves into her car.

"I hate when a guy can't take no for an answer," Maureen says as soon as Thaddeus is ensconced in the passenger seat.

"I can take no. I'm a salesman and I take no everyday. The only thing is it's hard to take a no after the kind of yes we had yesterday."

"I changed my mind."

"How come?"

"It's not right."

"It's as not right now as it was yesterday."

"Listen, it's not that I wouldn't want to, okay. I guess you know that."

"You ever been with a black guy before?"

"That's got nothing to do with it."

"You didn't answer my question."

"No, I never have. But that's not the reason. Don't give me any race stuff, okay? I don't like that. That's all you hear these days and I'm sick of it. People are people. A married guy is a married guy, dammit. I'm not curious about you because you're black. I know some girls these days are. That's not me."

"Then what are you?"

"I guess I sometimes get into where I think I can see the good side to a really bad person."

"Thanks."

"No, listen, like you come off one way but underneath there's another guy you don't even know about. You're really a kind of sensitive, sweet guy. I can tell by your eyes and the way you talk when you're not trying to prove something to the world. But then you get all charged up and all the bullshit starts and I get very sad and wish I could like shake you and say cut it out. Be yourself. You don't need all that crap. I'm sorry, am I hurting you?"

"No, go 'head . . ."

"It's sort of like I know you want to be the best salesman in the world but it's not going to happen with all that super-charged talk of yours. You need to relax more and use that really great sensitivity. That's the part of you I find attractive and maybe that's my hang-up too. Wanting to reform guys. Like my older sister keeps getting involved with hopeless alcoholics trying to get them to stop. Me, I hate drinkers but if a guy has something wrong with him and I think I can bring him out of it—like I'm his visiting nurse or something . . . hey, that's me."

Thaddeus was all set to start making moves on Maureen to break her down. But she's hit him hard with what she's saying. Sensitivity is softness and you don't become a blazing success by being soft but by being driven and hard. Yet there's a siren call that makes him not want to ignore it—maybe because she's saying it. Maybe she's more than just another girl. Maybe she's special.

"So where's that going to get me—this sensitivity of yours?" he asks.

"I don't know. It's not the right question to ask."

"Sure it is. I ain't nothing in this world without being a success. No worse than nothing. Just another black guy paying rent to live in a white man's world."

"You need to get over all that race shit, Thaddeus," Maureen tells him strongly. "Yeah, easy for me to say because I'm white, right? But you use it to keep you down. It's your own personal slave chain. Things are changing. Sure, things still aren't fair and all but you can still be a pretty happy and successful guy even though you're black. I know it's hard to believe. You'd rather think all your problems are caused by your race. Hell, I see plenty of white salesmen who are as messed up as you are so what's their excuse?"

"Okay, so what if I wasn't married? What if I left my wife? We don't get along you know. We thinking seriously of busting up."

"You ought to stay together for your kid's sake."

That hits home. Thaddeus was finding himself thinking about Maureen as more than another conquest but he would never leave his daughter.

"I don't like divorce," Maureen says. "I guess that's the Catholic side of me."

She's aware of the dichotomy of choosing a part of the religion she likes and ignoring other parts. Maureen's been having sex since she was fourteen, dutifully going to confession, and habitually never saying a word about her sexual activity until she told Father Stanhope, this real cute priest, who was probably gay so what a waste of a salacious seventeen-year-old confession. Her parents are married over thirty years and absolutely hate each other but she's glad they stayed together because she loves her brothers and sisters and feels she's a well-balanced person because she grew up in a stable home. She decries this thing where if you get pissed at your spouse you take off and do your own thing.

"So what do you people do when you're miserable with each other?" Thaddeus asks.

"We drink."

Thaddeus laughs. "You'd rather me be a damn hard-on killing alcoholic than a happy adulterer, is that right?"

She turns to him. "Look right now because we're not really involved, I don't have any particular reason to want you to be anything and I would like to keep it that way."

He kisses her tenderly on the lips. She moves away.

"Stop it." He comes after her, takes her hand, and starts kissing it. He leans down and kisses her thighs and then runs his face up and kisses her tummy, his head stuck between her body and the steering wheel.

"Okay, what do you prove," she says, battling to get away. "You can get me hot? Big deal. Okay, lean back. Come on. Seriously lean back—push that seat back."

"Damn, you gonna give me a blow job again? I want to fuck you, girl."

"This is like the sedative they give crazy guys in nut houses to calm them down."

Her mouth is like a velvet cave, her serpentine tongue slithering over every part of his dick. She lowers his pants and takes his balls in her hands and runs her finger along his scrotum and up behind his ass gently massaging his asshole with the tip of her finger. Then she inserts her finger gently in his asshole. He becomes alarmed because the feeling is pleasurable. This girl is goddamn subversive—first getting him to eat pussy, then putting her finger up his asshole plus all that sensitivity bullshit but it's a fleeting admonition because she has him in a state of unadulterated rapture. As he is coming, she inserts her finger deeper. Goddamn bitch is fucking him in the ass like a fairy as his stuff is shooting out of him like an artillery shell. Damn! Damn!

"Okay," she says. "Go back to your car. I'll see you tomorrow at work."

He ought to not let her get away with this shit. Bitch is in control!! But he finds himself opening the door, stepping out into the street, and watching her pull away.

Damn!

Chapter Six

"I think something's going on between me and the wife of that insurance guy," Jonathan tells Timothy. "Like it's under the surface but I think we're both aware of it. The last session . . . it was almost like a date. Nothing overt of course but . . . like she's real girly-girly and I'm real guy-guy."

"Talk to your supervisor," Timothy says. "Get off the case."

Here's what happened when Jonathan was hired. The head of the center is this big black guy, Dr. Leonard Warren. After paperwork completed, decisions made, he sits Jonathan down in his office and says, "You know why I got this job? I'm not even a shrink. They needed a black man to head this place and they could hardly find a black shrink in all Queens. I'm a pediatrician. But I took courses in pediatric psychology and . . . they liked my name."

"Your name?"

"Jewish Philanthropy—the people there . . . big opera fans. Leonard Warren, famous Met baritone. Dead. I'm a baritone too. Sing in the church choir. It was a natural."

"Um-huh."

"Now I'm going to be totally honest with you. You people who study psychology are into total, deep-down honesty, aren't you? I hope you can take it."

"Please, yes, of course."

"I want to build this center up and make something of it. It started in '64, a ragtag operation with a dribble of state funding. Then it got big in the sixties with the Great Society and all and then when Reagan got in they cut the hell out of us. We dribbled through the Clinton years. We hide from Bush because we're small. When I came in, I needed to build things up again. I got the big guys more involved. United Way, United Jewish Appeal, Jewish Philanthropy, more state funding, working on the Feds to fork over more. Crack epidemic gone but now we got pills. Crack was better for us because of the publicity—crime and violence leads to more funding. It's all public relations and spin these days. Work with the kids young before they get hooked on Percocet.

"Why am I knocking myself out like this? Frankly, I'm tired of having baby shit all over me, tired of calls in the middle of the night. I want to get deep into administration and not have to look at another dirty diaper or reassure another nervous mother about the quality of her baby's poop, know what I mean? You see I'm honest. I talk about my personal ambition. One day there's going to be an African American president of the United States, you know that? Hard to believe? Yeah, it's going to happen but it ain't going to be me, no sir—but one day you will see African American Surgeons General. A whole line of them, like Jewish heads of Internal Revenue. That could be me.

"Now I'm looking to take people along with me on this ride to the top. Could be you. Maybe yes, maybe no. We'll see. You're bright, articulate, and seem dedicated. You may have a great future in this kind of work so I'm going to give you the kind of brutal, frank orientation that you'd be wise to pay attention to in order to be a success here at this center. You don't have any real experience with African Americans, do you? I know you don't so I'm going to save you some painful trial and error. Okay?

"No Freudian gobbledygook here because African Americans think it's all bullshit. You tell a black man about the Oedipus complex, he wants to fuck his mother, he's apt to pull a knife on you. You tell a black woman she suffers from penis envy she'll laugh your ass back out to Long Island. Don't go into their childhood. Everyone you see here will have one thing in common—a bad childhood. They want to forget it, not delve into it. You must come on strong with African American families. You gotta stop drinkin', man. You gotta stop doing drugs, girl. We get you into a program. You don't pay anything; all you need is to stop what you doing and admit you all fucked-up in group sessions. Okay? We only get funded by the amount of fucked-up folks we shuffle in and out of programs, not by the amount of neurosis we help people work through. And watch out for those little bitch addicts. Some of them cute and they'll suck your dick right off your crotch for a day's fix. Another thing. You are young. Maybe you go off and do your little pot or blow shit through your nose with your little yuppie girlfriend and you think that's all cool. Maybe you are into the new morality or I should say the new amorality, which ain't all that new anyway. But here, in Jamaica, Queens, this is the old morality. No drugs. No illicit sex. No drinking. Stay in school. Get a job. Stay straight and do right. That's what we stand for. Jonathan, you step out of line and these days someone's liable to come along and sue our asses off. Now you ain't got shit . . . studying for your doctorate you don't have a dime's worth of malpractice insurance, so you fuck up and they get some lawyer on *our* case for a couple of million dollars and wind up settling for half and me, as head of this place, is the one who is blamed. You, of course, even though you ain't out a dime are out a career. Have to switch over to research—work with some white mice or something that you can't fuck or get high with. Am I being too subtle?"

"I can't talk to my supervisor," Jonathan laments to Timothy. "I'm on his shit list as it is. I'm like a cop who has to give out his quota of tickets. I can't get people into programs fast enough for him. You should see this place, the Jamaica Family Center. They flood into the place begging for real help, real therapy. I have incredible cases; a multiple personality disorder, a genuine Electra, a delusional—cases that warrant in-depth, yes, dare I say it, even Freudian analysis, but all Dr. Fucking Leonard Warren wants is to get them into a program. A neurotic who doesn't drink or take drugs is a wasted number to him. He is the most racist man I have ever met. To him, only the Jews are interestingly neurotic—African Americans simply drink, do drugs, and avoid responsibility. He doesn't want me to see anyone past ten sessions before they go into a program. It's numbers, numbers, not helping people.

"You want me to tell him I got a little hang-up with one of my clients and I want to switch with another therapist at the center? I've had five sessions with these people and after four more he expects me to get rid of them and go on to the next one. He's pissed that neither of them needs or qualifies for a program so far."

"What would happen if you told him that you had a thing for the wife?"

"I don't know, but it wouldn't be very good. I think he might fire me."

"So?"

"So? You know what it'd be like to get fired from the Jamaica Family Center? Like this is the lowest of the low. They are hard up for therapists. I did them the biggest favor to go work there—this A-student NYU white guy. If he cans me he'll not be silent about why. Nothing confidential with Dr. Leonard Warren. He sings about everyone. We all know everything about the hang-ups of every therapist there. Tell him I have a thing for one of the clients? Are you crazy? Whenever he sees her he preens like a peacock. Last time he oozed up to her, shook her hand, ignoring her husband of course, and oiled a little speech about his being the head of the center and if there is anything he can do for *her* please don't hesitate to ask. *Me* tell him there might be something subliminal going on. Are you kidding?"

"You know above all, you have a sacred trust as a therapist. Though shalt not stick thine dick into your client."

"I did not stick my dick into my client."

"Thou shalt not stick either your psychic dick or your physical dick into your client. You gave her mind a fuck. You stuck your fucking libido into her psyche and you had a little mental orgasm because her psyche quivered for you. You created an untenable situation. Don't you know that? Hey, man, that's textbook—Shrink 101. Now the honorable thing to do is to pull up your psychic pants. Get out. Fast! Off the case. Well?"

"I think I can go on being their counselor."

"You don't want to give her up?"

"That's not it . . . only."

"Go on."

"I can help. Now I know so much about them. No one else can come with the experience I've had with them."

"That's for damn sure. After you fuck her, you can say hey, no one knows more about her feelings about her slightly dumpy thighs than me so how can anyone else treat her."

Jonathan would like to say he's quite sure there is nothing dumpy about Beverly's thighs but doesn't dare.

"You know," Jonathan says, "you're perfectly right, but do you have to be so fucking conventional? You're supposed to be reviving R. D. Laing, so why can't you come up with a different slant on this age-old problem of wanting to make love with *she who shouldn't be made love to*. I might as well be seeing any old fuddy-duddy shrink. I chose you because I wanted something different and to the extent you burned my ass on racial attitudes I'm not disappointed so far except for now. You're acting like some sort of authoritarian in this matter and I must say I'm disappointed in you."

"Very good, Jonathan. Now honestly could you have done that before you started with me?"

"Don't patronize me!"

Timothy pauses. Should he? Sure, why not? "You know I had sex with a client once."

"You did?" Jonathan's delighted. "How was she?"

"It was a guy."

Jonathan recoils. Timothy notices.

"I guess we have to work on your homophobic attitudes."

"Please, I have enough on my plate. You? A guy?"

"He was moving away anyway and our relationship was going to end naturally. It was our last session and we had maybe a half hour to go and he offered to blow me. He just came out with it. 'Timothy, before I leave, I would like to blow you.' Just straight like that. He'd been wanting to for a long time and he had an idea I might be receptive. Well, at first, I felt jolted and insulted. I came up with the usual protective patter we therapists need to shelter ourselves but then I realized we had been developing a kind of rapport and I was curious. He was a big attractive guy—a committed homosexual who was suffering the strains of hiding in a very macho world—a professional major league baseball player no less. I sometimes would watch him on TV and once I saw him scratch his balls—you know the way some of them do—and that sort of titillated me. I'd been having dreams and erotic thoughts about him without even allowing myself to be cognizant of them. So I admitted my reciprocal feelings but told him I couldn't, in all conscience, do it during a session, but that when our relationship was over I'd meet him outside and we'd have this one-time thing. I was satisfied with myself. I could control the situation. He said I was beginning to sound like a bad psychological novel. For a baseball player he was surprisingly erudite. Then he got up, locked my office door, sat down, yanked his big cock out and started to stroke it."

"What did you do?"

"I did the same thing. It was sort of a homosexual ritual. So we just sat looking at each other stroking our cocks. It was amazing. I'd never seen anything erotic about a guy's cock before—proud to be the world's most committed hetero—but there I was sitting where I'm sitting now and he was sitting there where you're sitting. Don't get nervous, Jonathan."

"Please!"

"Anyway, we were getting hard at the same time. Then he stood up and hovered over me for a second and I could have died because I was afraid he'd try to kiss me but instead, intuiting my fear, he simply got on his knees and started to skillfully play with me. Well, let me tell you something, I have no idea of your oral sex history—after all we've hardly gone into such detail—but before this guy I thought I was the expert on blow jobs. I thought this one girl from sunny Spain with a mouth as wide as the Iberian Peninsula was the most unbeatable practitioner in the world, but I was wrong. You need to get you a homosexual to really get the job done the way it ought to be done. Yes, I did it to him too. And you know what? It was not so terrible or disgraceful though I immediately discerned, with some sense of relief, that I had not found my life's work. Am I now living up to my radical therapist credential?

"This experience helped me define where my true erotic self lies. Women, thank you. Actually women with very little tit and high cheekbones like my current little Suzy Highfoot."

"Your true erotic self? What does that mean?"

"We all have that which turns us on the most. Oh, sure, all pretty women, all attractive, breasts a certain way . . . perhaps an overbite, or perhaps in some cases . . . dark skin and an ass that scoops out from the spine and hangs up high. You cannot have a truly satisfying erotic life without your mate possessing such features."

Jonathan thinks of Dorothy Dandridge and then Beverly. Creamy brown skin, a perfectly formed, high-cheekbone face. Slim, wickedly lithe body.

"So what are you telling me in all this?" Jonathan asks.

"You're in a precarious situation. Do not act on your impulses in this case or it can prove disastrous. That's the conventional me."

"And the other?"

"Who the hell knows what the other is saying. It might be the best thing you ever did."

"Thank you for all this clarity."

"Our time is up now."

The session with Thaddeus, Beverly, and Jonathan is, so far in the opening moments, quite barren. Subtext is pervasive.

Jonathan asks how things have been going. Thaddeus says everything's been okay. No major fights or problems. Beverly agrees, yes things have been calm.

Beverly's been profoundly moved and confused by her last session. She feels the enchantment of being at the threshold of self-knowledge, realizing she's been leading a life propelled by blind instinct with no real insight into her own behavior. She's enthralled with her future journey yet she's not quite sure if her new pursuit has anything to do with Jonathan's interest in her and hers in him. Is she showing off for him—the way any ditzy female would who, say, bones up on baseball because her boyfriend is a great fan? She played that game with Sheldon but she knew then it was only a game. But that was when she was carefree, no problems, no oppressive husband and needy child in her life. It's different now. She sees where her shallowness has taken her.

What can she say with Thaddeus here? He's such an intruder. She just needs to get through this session so she can be alone with Jonathan again but she finds it difficult to conceive of waiting for their individual session. Maybe she can call him and they can speak on the phone.

Thaddeus doesn't care what happens during these joint sessions. He'd really like to open up to this dude about all this Maureen stuff. Get his head straight because that bitch has not only been playing with his dick but his head as well. Damn what can he talk about with Bitch Beverly in the room?

The solution to Jonathan's problem hits him with a mental thump. He simply has to be perfectly honest. He has to admit that he has developed a countertransference problem and needs to remove himself from the case—like a judge if the case he's assigned involves his brother-in-law or former law partner. It's a simple matter of ethics. He clears his throat to tell them he's going to bow out and assign them to another therapist. When they ask why, he will simply take a breath and admit he's developed . . . feelings around . . . Mrs. Carmichael . . . feelings that really make it most difficult to be objective.

What feelings? Thaddeus will ask, his face clouding up.

Jonathan's suddenly afraid Thaddeus might have a knife. They all carry knives. Why did he come down here to Jamaica in the first place to be a marriage counselor? His mother had said, "Marriage counseling? With all the *schvatza?* They don't have marital unions there, they have encounters that create children. Then the guys take off and the gals go on welfare. Who needs counseling for that? Are you going to tell the guy how to hide from his obligations and the girl how to apply for welfare? They know that already. It's bred in the bone. White people have problems. Jews have problems. Whenever you want to stick together to create and perpetuate a family there are problems because people weren't meant to be together for the long pull. In the caves it was in and out and on to the next cave. You know, maybe the *schvatza* have the right idea. You think after I got to know your father really well, that *momser,* I would have stayed with him if it wasn't for the children? No way. Same him with me. He figured he was marrying a hot tomato and instead he got a cold pancake. You're messing with these poor people. Right now they're happy. They drink, they screw around. No responsibilities on the job—like if you're a janitor, what do you worry about? Counseling? Could lead to buying houses on our block. Then they have to worry about taxes and crabgrass and Dominicans moving in. Counseling? This is like the missionaries bringing religion to Africa along with all the European diseases. These people are happy in their ghettos. And frankly I'm happy too. So I pay a little more in taxes for all the people on welfare in Freeport. Big deal. The only *schvatza* I want to see is the one cleaning my floor. I don't want no *schvatza* dentist looking down my throat or no *schvatza* doctor sticking his fingers you know where. Counseling? Better a nice Jewish boy should maybe, God forbid, take the test for sanitation than be a counselor for the *schvatza* in Jamaica, Queens."

Jonathan cannot be perfectly honest. Another solution comes with another thud. It's better! He goes with it, blurts it out quickly, instinctively before something rational comes along to dissuade him. "I'm afraid I'm going to be leaving this . . . position . . ." he stammers.

A vast silence. Then, "What"? Thaddeus stunned.

Tears spring to Beverly's eyes.

"I'll see to it you're assigned a top-notch therapist," Jonathan says, hating the bullshit because he hasn't run across any top-notch therapists so far at the Jamaica Family Center. Actually he thinks of himself as the most brilliant one there and look how fucked-up he is. Now he feels an enormous wave of relief. It's over!! He knows now he wants to work in minority centers like this one—overcome any vestige of racial provincialism that still remains. There are so many that need him—Freeport, Roosevelt, Harlem, Bed-Stuy. He'll find a center where they believe in truly working with clients rather than simply shuffling them off into programs!

The Sale Doesn't Begin Until The Prospect Says No. One of the greatest books on sales ever written. Thaddeus immediately recognizes that the sales process has geared into its second stage. The first is the presentation of a potentially attractive idea. Do you want your retirement to be totally carefree? Wouldn't you like your family taken care of in the event of your untimely death? Now, here, in Jonathan's case, wouldn't you like to climb into bed with this unbelievable-looking woman? The prospect has considered this temptation and it is so powerful it causes a tumultuous negative reaction. Great!

"I have no idea how my wife feels about what you've just told us," Thaddeus says quietly. "But frankly I'm devastated. You have no idea how much you've helped me so far."

Jonathan almost wants to leave his seat and grab Thaddeus's arm to reassure him about . . . something or other but can't think what. His mouth drops open and the clichés about being able to quickly establish a rapport with another therapist and the fact that they've only had a few sessions expire before they can be uttered.

He hasn't dared look at Beverly yet. When he does he finds tears streaming down her face. She suddenly stands up and runs from the office.

"How can you do this to us, man?" Thaddeus asks woefully.

Where did Beverly go? What might she do? Was he a fool to spring this on her like that? He has no extensive knowledge of her background—can't predict how she might react to his announcement. There's a procedure for leaving a client—a gradual pullback, some notice, a session or two of working feelings out—separation anxiety, feelings of abandonment. He suddenly thinks of all the traffic on Jamaica Avenue, Beverly running across the street in tears, not looking where she's going.

"W-where do you think she went?" he asks Thaddeus.

"I don't know, man."

"Don't you think you should . . . like check where she is?" Jonathan asks.

Thaddeus shrugs his I don't give a shit shrug. Then visibly broods. Get the quixotic side to this motherfucka going. Yeah, man, I don't give a shit if she gets hit by the downtown bus, raped by the Boston Strangler, hacked up with a Texas chainsaw.

Jonathan rises and leaves the office. Luella Peters stares at him with big, brown, amazed eyes. Jonathan doesn't care. He's leaving this place anyway. Fuck Luella Peters. Fuck Dr. Leonard Warren. He dashes for the ladies room and knocks on the steel door.

"Mrs. Carmichael, Beverly . . . are you all right?" he shouts through the door. No one can hear through this goddamn prison door! He opens it a crack, averting his eyes obviously lest someone accuse him of perversity. The door is pulled back and he is facing a very fat, black lady.

"Is there a lady in there . . . crying or something?" Jonathan asks her.

"There's one shooting up in one booth and another seems like she's having a miscarriage in another," the fat lady says. "Neither of 'em crying though."

Jonathan moves down the stairs too impatient to wait for the ponderous elevator. Beverly is in the lobby leaning against a corner huddled over a tissue and crying.

Jonathan moves to her. "Mrs. Carmichael," he says. "Beverly . . ."

She turns her back and cries against the faux marble wall. He reaches out to touch her shoulder but stops. Looks around. There are people coming in and out of the building all the time but so far no one seems to be paying attention. Does he dare touch her shoulder? He wants her to understand but understand what?

"I . . . I'm sorry . . . I really am . . . " he stammers.

Thaddeus has taken the elevator down and when he gets off he spots the scene near the front of the lobby. He tucks himself into a corner and watches.

Now she stares directly at Jonathan. There's a defiant pleading look to her. Jonathan feels his heart is going to break.

"You don't understand, do you?" she says. "How can you do this?"

"I have to work on my doctoral . . ."

"And me? You'll have no more contact with me?"

"You'll have another . . ."

"You know what I mean."

He doesn't dare form an image of what she means.

Then Dr. Leonard Warren moves into the building. He stops and stares at the scene. The loveliest client the Jamaica Family Center ever had crying against a wall and her so-called therapist leaning into her. Why if one didn't know any better one might think . . .

"Is everything all right here?" Dr. Warren asks, peering closely at Beverly. "Mrs. Carmichael, are you all right?"

Jonathan sees Thaddeus with an indignant, belligerent look marching toward them.

"May I speak to you a moment Dr. Warren?" Thaddeus blares out. People in the lobby turn and stare. "I don't think it's fair just because we are . . . to play with our minds this way," Thaddeus orates. "Shuffle us from therapist to therapist just when we are building a rapport. No transition. No regard for our feelings! Would this kind of thing happen over there on Park Avenue in New York City?!"

"What are you talking about?" Dr. Warren asks.

"Just when we are on the verge of pouring our hearts and souls out to this man he ups and tells us he's going to leave."

Jonathan has handled this like a real *schmuck*. He needed to speak to Warren first and then the clients. He's going to get his ass reamed and a lousy report. His therapeutic career off on the wrong foot. Warren knows everyone in New York State. Jonathan's name will be shit!

"No, I was starting to say . . . and perhaps it didn't come out right . . . or you jumped to conclusions . . . anyway I started to say that I would leave . . . eventually," Jonathan says.

Beverly stops crying and begins to smile radiantly. A wave of happiness engulfs Jonathan before another wave of despair gets him. That smile. That luminescence in her eyes. Is he doomed!?

"I meant, but it didn't come out right, that someday I'd have to leave, like when I needed to really sit down and write my thesis and stuff . . ."

"We jumped to the wrong conclusion then," Thaddeus says. "Hear that, honey? We jumped to the wrong conclusion. We always do that, don't we? That's one of our problems that your Mr. Meltzer here is helping us with. He's the greatest!"

Dr. Warren peers from one to the other of them. Some shit going on here.

"Well, then we still have some time left in the session, don't we?" Thaddeus says. He places himself on one side of Jonathan and Beverly places herself on the other and they walk toward the elevator with Dr. Warren a couple of steps ahead of them. Jonathan is a prisoner. He peers up at the large arrow of the elevator as it descends—a kind of slow guillotine, his neck in its path. The elevator door opens, Dr. Warren gallantly steps aside for Beverly, and they march in, turn around, and face the doors as they slide shut. Jonathan now thinks of the doors of hell closing on him. He's being put up against the wall of his own desires while his duty moves in and pulverizes him. He blinks and looks about. They all know it. The black man's revenge. They've captured this little white boy in the heart of Africa and are leading him to a big kettle where they are going to roast his lily-white Jew ass and have him for breakfast, lunch, and dinner. He's cooked.

Chapter Seven

"Man," Thaddeus leans across Jonathan's desk poking at his forearm, "bitch is playing with my head."

"Beverly?"

"No, not the wife. I mean this other bitch, Maureen."

"What's going on?" Jonathan leans back and puts his hands on top of his head a moment, catches himself, and brings his hands down.

"I don't know where to begin. It's scary, you know. Bitch . . . I guess I ought to stop calling her that cause she's really not a bitch. She just knows me so well—knows all my attitudes and pretensions and can see through them. It bothers me because I do have an act, you know—like a comedian's routine . . . without his routine he ain't funny anymore. Sometimes I think that's all there is. There's no real me to *be* so I need to *be* something—this pushy guy who thinks of everything in some artificial way—trying to be super salesman and blaming every failing in life on race. She says to me that hey, it's possible to be a nice happy guy even if you're black. There's plenty of injustice in the world but even so you can be happy. That hit me."

"Why does that have such a strong effect on you?"

"I don't know. I suppose I've heard it before from other people—maybe even other girls I've been with, maybe even Beverly sometimes when she's taking off at me for the way I'm behaving and shit. But it's the first time it really hit me hard, I suppose, because, I see myself getting older and life slipping by and I see the mistakes my comedy routine has already led me into. Plus I think I'm beginning to feel something for her, Maureen, like I never felt about any other woman before. Like she's a good-looking woman sure, but no prize like Beverly, but she looks you right in the eye and tells you how she feels about you. She's trying to get me to become a more sensitive, caring person because I think she feels she might love me if I was that way and I guess I do want her to love me because I guess . . . oh shit . . . I guess I'm in love with her. I don't know though, I'm confused. I can't really make rational, honest decisions. But you know what? As I'm talking to you I see this has been the most honest I have ever been in my entire life."

"How does that make you feel? Right now?"

"Good. But scared."

Thaddeus has a pang of conscience because Jonathan is really a good counselor and there he is plotting against the guy. But he chooses to ignore his conscience.

Beverly is moving closer to Jonathan—the way she dresses for the sessions, the way she looks, talks, walks. She's on the prowl and the strike is near. Jonathan's about to be snared. It hasn't happened yet, Thaddeus instinctively knows, but when it does he'll have to figure out how to handle exposing it. He's already spoken to a lawyer, Morris Lieberman, whom he used when he claimed a neck injury in a car accident a couple of years ago.

"You don't need to prove this kind of thing beyond a reasonable doubt," Morris Lieberman told him. "But you do need some strong enough stuff so that they'll settle without too much fuss. But let me ask you something, how does that make you feel about your wife and your marriage counselor?"

"It's like she ain't my wife anymore, just some bitch making my life miserable. I'll give her some of the damn settlement so she's going to benefit too. When we part I want her to raise my daughter right. Get out of that damn neighborhood, get her a house on Long Island, and send Janelle to a good white school. Bitch gets herself fucked and some money besides—what harm am I doing her? Right now ain't nobody fucking her, far as I know, and she certainly got no money. She get herself another guy in no time, maybe even the marriage counselor, that sucker's hooked on her . . . except I know how you people feel if one of you comes home with one of us."

"Little Moishe Levine is stationed in Fort Bragg, Georgia. He calls home one day and his mother gets on the phone."

Morris Lieberman, like most lawyers, has a vast repertoire of jokes to cover any and all occasions. "Ma, I met the most wonderful person in the world."

"A girl?"

"Yes, mom, of course."

"Thanks God!"

"I love her and . . . we got married."

"*Oy*, I'm *kvelling*. I'm overjoyed! What is this wonderful girl's name? Tell me so I can make a prayer to God so that you both can have joy and happiness for a hundred years."

"Her name is Leticia."

"Leticia . . ."

"Now the only thing is mom . . . well . . . we made a little mistake."

"A little mistake?"

"Yeah, we should have waited but . . . Leticia is . . . pregnant."

"Pregnant?"

"Yeah, and they discharged me from the army those anti-Semites."

"Why?"

"I punched an officer because he made a racial slur."

"A racial slur?"

"God I hate to even say it . . . he called Leticia a nigger."

"Why would he call someone that?"

"Well, because Leticia is . . . African American."

"Colored?"

"African American, Mother."

"Oh . . ."

"Mom, we need to come home to have the baby. Do you think you can make some room for us in the apartment until we can afford a place of our own?"

"You can have my room."

"Your room? Where are you going to sleep?"

"No problem. After this phone call I'm dropping dead."

Thaddeus is beginning to look forward to these private sessions with Jonathan. There are times, as now, where he would like to just tell Jonathan what he has in mind for him but he doesn't. Where would that leave him?

"Is there anything else on your mind?" Jonathan asks.

"No . . . nothing really."

"Sometimes the fleeting thought can be the one we want to pursue."

"That's slick."

"It's more than slick, it's true. How are things going with you and Beverly? You don't talk very much about her anymore."

"She's there man—just there. Let me ask you something. How would you feel if you couldn't save this marriage? If we got divorced and shit."

"I'm here to help you both find the right path, wherever that might lead."

"You wouldn't be like disappointed?" Thaddeus probes. "Like you didn't do your job?"

"Why are you so concerned about my feelings?"

"Why not? Isn't that part of the therapeutic process—to wonder how the seemingly objective counselor is really reacting?" Thaddeus replies.

"Yes, it is. Actually if you went to one of the more radical counselors, you'd be dealing with their head as well as your own."

"Is that the one you go to?" Thaddeus asks.

"Yes, it's part of my training."

"Have you ever talked about us . . . me and Beverly?"

"Yes, I have."

"As part of talking about all your clients?" Thaddeus probes.

Jonathan smiles. "You want to know what I say about you, right?"

"Sure."

"That's as confidential as I keep your material," Jonathan replies.

"I knew you'd say that."

"What else can I say?"

"You could be honest."

"I am being honest."

"No, you're simply not being dishonest. There's a difference, isn't there?" Thaddeus replies.

"Are you being honest with me? After all, in our roles it's you who are supposed to be completely forthright and it's me who has an obligation to be selective in what I reveal."

"Why do you feel I'm not completely forthright?"

Jonathan takes a chance. "I . . . feel you have certain feelings about your wife and . . . me . . . that you aren't revealing."

"It seems you and Beverly have a . . . nice relationship."

"Nice?"

"Nice . . . therapeutic relationship. She seems to trust you and look forward to seeing you, especially alone. It's close to the way I feel about seeing you alone. I hate these joint sessions where I have to think of all this domestic bullshit to bring up. The real meat is in the individual sessions and I suspect she feels that way too. I don't even know why we need these joint sessions anyway."

"Um-huh."

"Let me ask you something a little strange. If me and Beverly broke up would you . . ." he can't be too shockingly crude for the white boy so he says . . . "date her?"

"Date her?"

"You know I sort of feel sorry for you. A fine bitch like Beverly coming here telling all her secrets and shit. You ain't made of stone, are you? She's real nice if she's treated nice. I think sometimes I bring out the worst in her. Like I could see you two dating. This is a new age, man. Jew don't have to be with Jew and black with black. We all brothers and sisters."

"So if you and Beverly break up you'd like me to hook up with her?"

"Sure, man, why not?"

"Are you attempting to soothe your guilt over the idea of leaving her by trying to find her a suitable replacement?"

"That's right! Ain't I the nice guy?! Some guys just leave the bitch and fuck her—let her go on welfare—but here I am trying to fix her up with a good guy, going to be a doctor with a good future. What do you think?"

"Do you think I'd be a good stepfather to your little daughter?"

"Hell, yeah, bring her up with some solid Jewish values. Make sure any dude she gets involved with has a good education or his father a good business. Teach her to not spread for no dude unless she gets a ring first. Don't do your own housework, get you a *schvatza*. Hell, yeah, best thing I could do for my little girl is get her out of the ghetto, into Long Island, brought up as a double JAP—JamaicanJewish American Princess. Hot damn."

Thaddeus has veered too close to his scheme so he spends the rest of the session speaking about his negative feelings about being a salesman.

During the rest of the session Jonathan holds off examining the feelings elicited by Thaddeus's matchmaking. When Thaddeus leaves—no smarmy handshake this time. Jonathan takes a moment to allow domestic images of being married to Beverly float through his mind before the next session begins. But the images blur and oscillate with anxiety. It's her color, not her beauty, that infuses the images with fear. He calls his next client.

⟿

Jonathan has begun to tell Arlene about the Carmichaels. At one point, feeling so secure and comfortable, he even tells Arlene about his Beverly fantasy.

"Dorothy Dandridge was a catalyst for me too," Arlene tells Jonathan. "It's like you talk about Carmen Jones but to me it was *Porgy and Bess*. I mean there I was this young, little Jewish kid with all my other Jewish kid friends on Pelham Parkway and I see this movie on TV where this totally beautiful black girl is so worried about being touched by this big black guy Crown—remember him?—because once he touches her, just touches her, mind you, she's a goner. And like I kept wondering what that meant. I mean a guy lays a hand on you and you are lost? Like maybe I'm fourteen or something and starting to wonder about guys and this whole concept comes along about being a goner if a certain guy touches you in a certain way or something like that. Soon I realized I wanted to be a goner too in some certain sense. I knew I was going to get a good education and be a professional woman so I felt safe. I could tell I was sort of like my mother and sister, you know, not too hot—sort of sour on the physical side of things and more into what guys are supposed to do for you in material ways. So I would get crushes on guys and I'd get real aggressive getting them to touch me. I thought I had a little red button hidden on me somewhere and these guys were like search parties. But it didn't work. I would have sex and it would be okay . . . sort of, but I was never close to being a 'goner.'

"I started to ride my bike near the Kingsbridge section, the black neighborhood, and I watched how the kids moved and talked. The girls especially—so many of them were like Dorothy Dandridge, not as beautiful of course, but in the way they moved and acted. Most black girls are wanton—even if their asses are fat and their tits sag, they go around being sexy. And then one day this black kid, maybe twenty years old—not real cute but wicked looking—stood in front of my bicycle and stopped me cold and squinted at me and I started feeling like a goner. I peddled away quick. Scared but real happy in a sense because I knew I was capable of that feeling. Fluttery inside, helpless . . . and then there were the juices. Wet. Like really wet. I'd been having sex for maybe a year and mostly it hurt because there was no lubrication and here I have this little encounter and a car axle could have gone up there and it would've been a smooth ride. I was very troubled. I kept away for a long time but then I started to ride my bike again. A lot of these black guys really turned me on. If you think about it in even the most obvious ways, you know the jungle . . . forbidden fruit and all that crap . . . it's really right there. And then I saw that wicked-looking kid hanging out with a bunch of guys and he saw me and I could tell I was in his head too. And then it was wild, I mean me, little Arlene from Pelham Parkway. This kid is putting my bike under the stairs in his apartment building and we're going up to the roof. They got old mattresses and chairs up there and there's a couple of his friends smoking pot and I take a hit and get a little high and soon his friends leave and we start to get it on and I am so fucking thrilled with myself, popping all over the place. I could not get enough of him—his name was Clarence—like I wanted to eat him up alive. I used to go around there all the time for about six months till he got busted for drugs and sent to Green Haven."

They're in bed in Arlene's new apartment, which she's sharing with two other NYU graduate students, Craig who is gay, and Julie who is Midwest. Arlene's into the expansive side of her pot and Jonathan's hazily drifting with a 'lude.

"So do you think about Clarence when you're having sex? Is that why you're always so hot?" Jonathan says stupidly.

Arlene sneers at him. "Once the skill is learned it's like riding a bike. I'm thinking of doing my thesis on Female Jewish Frigidity—The Myth and Reality."

"What's the myth?"

"Very funny. If all Jewish women are supposed to be frigid how come I'm not?"

"You had to work at it. You needed a dose of jungle fever. You know over there at the Jamaica Center we treat every ill imaginable except one—frigidity. We've never had a case of a woman complaining about it or a man, for that matter, not able to get it up for any other reason except alcohol or drugs.

Their problem is the other way around—they're too goddamn turned on for their own good. Too many babies and too many sex partners. They could use a dose of good ol' Jewish frigidity just like those goddamn JAPs out in Long Island could use a dose of jungle fever."

"There is no evidence of frigidity in Biblical times," says Arlene. "Actually there's ample evidence of passion and fecundity. The trouble starts when the Jews are expelled from the Promised Land. They are despised, ghettoized, and persecuted. In essence they lose their masculinity. They are castrated—it's not their fault of course. They've been dealt a raw deal but women do not see things that way. So here are all these Jewish guys and instead of protecting and hunting they stick their noses in books, become religious scholars, tell the women they're really like second-class citizens. The guys become usurers and tailors while the woman work their butts off on stinking little farms while raising the kids waiting in fear for the Cossacks to come along and burn them out while their pious husbands can only moan and pray to a God who doesn't do shit for them."

"You're right," Jonathan says. "I don't care what the modern woman tells you but they really want warriors and hunters. Look at those butchy-bitchy sabra women in Israel. They can't come enough. Why? Because Israeli guys are tough. Sabras don't go to shrinks because they can't get orgasms. The sabras might have to go to doctors because they're getting too many orgasms—on buses, bicycles . . . maybe on the firing range and shit."

Arlene gets out of bed and goes to the small bathroom. When she comes back she says, "Now for you, young man, your problem with this married couple is totally clear to me."

"Oh?"

"You're involved in trying to work through your homo-sexual feelings over the guy."

"What are you talking about?"

"It's been obvious to me for a long time that you are a repressed homosexual."

"I'm a repressed homosexual?"

"You didn't know that? It's never come up in your analysis?"

Jonathan thinks. "You know I have just been objectively reviewing every thought I have ever had. I've gone back to thoughts and images in the womb, infancy, preadolescence, adolescence, manhood. I can now safely tell you I have never, never, never, never had one homosexual image, urge, thought—fleeting or otherwise."

"You've just proven my point," Arlene replies. "You have repressed it perfectly. Can't you see you really want to get it on with this Carmichael guy? Can't you see when you saw him with this white chick in front of your office you were incredibly turned on by the guy?"

"This is so absurd. Arlene, you of all people should be able to testify to my heterosexuality."

"Your homosexuality has been obvious to me from the very get-go."

Jonathan flushes and clenches his fist. Thank God they are in the dark and she doesn't see how much she's hurt him. He's going to break up with her. Fuck her. Ugly big-titted, oversexed Jewish cow!

"You feel your cock is too small—you don't think I know that?" Arlene is crouching in front of him trying to get him to look at her. She's gone through this kind of thing with guys before and afterward they never want to see her again but that's all right. This is the crucible she puts guys through. If any of them can ever endure she'll consider marrying them.

"That's ridiculous, my cock's not too small," Jonathan mutters. "Is it?"

"What could it be too small for?"

"What do you mean?"

"To have sex with a woman a guy's cock can be almost any size. You know that. Our cunts are like Spandex—one size fits all. God is a man."

"How do you know that?"

"Because he built women for disappointment and men for gratification. He gives us eleven to thirteen inches of tunnel and you guys anywhere from four to eight of dick—that means unless we fuck the biggest dude in Harlem we always have five to nine inches of unfulfilled, empty, yearning space. If God was a woman she'd have made our cunts two inches deep so that you bastards could have two, three, four, or five inches always out in the cold. But that's okay. We always have to settle.

"But, anyway, you, Mr. Jonathan Meltzer, are so worried about the size of your cock because it's a homosexual obstacle course. Big dick, flat stomach, tight ass. You of course have never looked at a guy's dick in a locker room and compared it to your own, have you? No, not you."

And then it floods in on him—all the times he has peeked at guys in a locker room comparing. But had he been peeking for any other reason? Then he thinks about Thaddeus with that girl in the car and about his shrink with that baseball player and then Arlene says, "Then there's this premature ejaculation thing."

"Oh?"

"Which shortens the heterosexual lovemaking process. It's so apparent."

"What should I do about all this then?"

"Stop repressing. Get it on with the guy or if that's not practical there's my roommate Craig who thinks you're real cute."

"You want me to get it on with Craig?"

"If you want to."

"And you?"

"Oh, me, I've already started exploring my homosexuality."

"Julie Midwest?"

"She's sweet."

"And?"

"And what?"

"What are you?"

"Human."

"Oh, so all humans are bisexual?"

"Yes, of course, you didn't know that and going to be a doctor yet."

"You know, Arlene, I hate to say this but I think you're an awful bitch."

"Go on. I lose more guys this way. Go on. Tell me off."

"I don't have to tell you anything."

Jonathan is getting dressed to go. Arlene relights her joint. "Don't let the door hit you in the ass on your way out," she says, as Jonathan is about to leave.

Too bad she kind of likes him. If he comes back she'll get him to marry her. She's twenty-eight and it's about time. She wonders how it would feel to make love to a woman. Certainly not Julie Midwest but someone more cosmopolitan but she can think of no one and besides the idea actually repels her. She made up that guy Clarence on the roof story on the spot so she could relate to poor Jonathan and his tawdry obsession. She finds it sadly hilarious that guys are so ready to believe all Jewish women are cold.

Actually the *schmuck* brought it all on himself. There he is with her and she's screwing his head off, servicing him beautifully, so why then does the little putz tell her about his hots for this other woman. He's got some fucking nerve!

Thaddeus waits for Luella Peters to emerge from the building for her lunch break. When she does, he walks up behind her and scoops her elbow up in his hand.

"Oh! It's you, you scared me," she giggles. "You never know when someone's going to try to snatch your purse in this neighborhood."

"How you doin', baby? Goin' out for lunch?"

"Just for a little tea and toast." Luella's always on a diet until it comes to actually ordering and then instead of tea and toast, it's a BLT with mayo and a Coke.

"Come on, baby, it's on me," Thaddeus urges, squeezing her unbelievably soft elbow. Damn, woman's elbow feels like a breast.

"Oh no, you don't have to do that," Luella gushes coyly.

"Oh, come on, girl."

Luella allows herself to be guided to the corner diner. She greets the owner and a waitress behind the counter effusively, "Hello Dimitri, oh, hi Thelma, how you doin' baby?" She's all aflutter because she's with Thaddeus who looks extra sharp this afternoon in a dark beige suit with a bright green tie, carrying a briefcase so alligator it looks like it's about to snap your hand off. They slide into a rounded booth toward the rear where they sit thigh by thigh.

Luella whispers in Thaddeus's ear, giving him a whiff of something so sickeningly sweet it comes close to making him nauseous, "You know I maybe shouldn't be seen with a client of the center."

He's plugged big mommas before and can attest to their worthiness once in the sack, so grateful to have a slim young dude twixt their legs they perform in a high and mighty style. He can well understand how it was in those golden olden days when this kind of shape was considered the sexiest because there's so much more of everything everywhere.

"Why is that, darling?" Thaddeus asks.

"Well, I don't know except Dr. Warren has strict rules about that kind of thing." This uttered as if she's a fourteen-year-old virgin back in ol' Spain or something sneaking behind her chaperone's back.

"Well, that's only for therapists and clients, isn't it?"

"I suppose."

"And besides I don't think all the therapists abide by those rules."

The waitress comes by and Luella is reluctantly forced to order tea and toast while Thaddeus orders a BLT with mayo.

"What did you mean, sweetie?" Luella asks pointedly, when the waitress departs.

"Mean?"

"Yeah, just now with that remark about not all the therapists abiding by the rules."

Thaddeus clasps her kneecap firmly in his hand and stares into her eyes.

"I'm haunted."

"Haunted?"

Tears appear at the corners of his eyes.

"I don't know if I can say it. I don't even want to think about it, baby. It's killing me inside."

"Are we thinking about the same thing, sweet child?"

Luella stares deeply into Thaddeus's eyes. She clasps her hands on Thaddeus's and moves it up her fleshy leg an inch or so.

"I think we are," Thaddeus says. "Damn!" Thaddeus brings his free hand up to cover his eyes. Luella moves his hand on her leg up farther. Thaddeus squeezes her upper thigh.

"It ain't right, baby!" Luella says emphatically. "It ain't right."

"If I could only know for sure," Thaddeus says, clenching his fist.

"What would you do? Nothing violent, would you?"

"No, sweet woman, no, that ain't my nature. I would seek justice and retribution in a civilized way. I would reluctantly have to sue the center."

"Yes, you should do that. Sue their ass."

"But the only thing." Thaddeus now three-quarters up her thigh. "I need proof, sweet momma."

"But are you sure?"

"I know my wife. I know that woman."

"Oh, Lord . . . oh Lord . . . I was afraid . . . sometimes when she passes me after a session with him I can almost smell it on her. You know what I mean?"

"Yeah, yeah, when she gets home, me too. The woman hummin' and purrin' but not for me."

"That woman stupid. If I had me something like you to come home to I would never, never go astray."

"You so good. You so nice."

"I hate that! You know that! I'm sorry, she your wife and I know you love her and all but she nothin' but a damn hussy baby—got to face it."

"Oh, God."

"Listen, baby, you in need of comfortin'." Luella leans into Thaddeus.

"Yeah, yeah . . ."

"You want to take me someplace after work? I'm what you need, baby, right now. Right now, hear. You let your Aunt Luella take care of you, okay, baby?"

"Yeah, baby, yeah . . ."

Their order appears. "You come by here at four thirty. Maybe we can figure something out together," Luella says, biting into her unsatisfactory toast. Don't make no difference, she thinks, I'm gonna be partaking of something more tasty later on.

Beverly perches demurely on her chair. "Where do you live?" she asks.

"Merrick, Long Island," Jonathan replies.

"Is that a nice town?"

"Oh, yes, it's very nice."

"You have your own house or apartment there?"

"No, I don't. My parents," he mumbles. "I live with my parents. Brother and sister too."

"Oh?"

"Well, I don't make much . . . until I get my doctorate and start my own practice . . ."

"Do you have your own separate apartment with a separate entrance?" she asks.

"Yes."

"Um-huh."

"Here I am almost thirty and I still depend on my parents. I should get a small apartment in the city—maybe share it or something. My mother is the worst . . ." He doesn't want to go into her bigotry so he skips that. "When I get my doctorate and go into practice my income will be . . ." instead of saying okay he says . . . "quite substantial." Beverly's eyes brighten. "Then I'll get a nice place but my therapist says I'm copping out. Not growing up. Too dependent on mummy and daddy. I don't even have my own car. I don't even use my own credit card."

"Oh? Whose credit card do you use?"

"My father's American Express."

"Oh?"

"I took a girl to a motel once and my father made sure to tell my mother about it because he saw it on the bill. She put me through a big third degree about who the girl was and then she made me go to our family doctor to make sure I hadn't caught anything."

He's aware he's falling headlong into a Timothy imitation. He's really going too far with it. Yet he has trouble stopping because Beverly is such a commanding audience, leaning forward, eating up details.

"Had you?"

"No, of course not. I'm very responsible when it comes to . . ."

"Um-huh."

"Are you sure you want to hear any more of this?"

Beverly's right at the home she loves to be in. Jonathan is so much like Sheldon. Sheldon could go on and on about all his hang-ups and she loved it.

"I suffer from premature ejaculation," Jonathan says. He's crazy. He can't believe he said that!

Beverly has to think about what he's now talking about. The last thing she wants is to appear ignorant. Premature? That's too soon. Ejaculation? Oh, that. She never heard of a man admitting to that. They usually roar like lions even though they wind up performing like jackasses.

"Um-huh," Beverly manages to say. A new symbol implants itself into her mind. American Express. Oh, sure it's not his card but it's in the family. When Jonathan gets to be a man, that'll be the credit card of his choice because it's the one he's accustomed to. If it's his choice then won't it be the choice of his future . . . ?

"You know I find your openness refreshing," she says. "A typical Jamaican man won't even cover a wound if it's bleeding; never admit to any weakness at all even if it's exceedingly apparent. Sheldon was like that too. He told me about homosexual tendencies. Can you believe a guy would tell that to a girl? At first I was shocked but then I liked it. Not his homosexual tendencies, which couldn't have been all that bad, but the fact he would come out with it. And now as you started to talk about this premature thing . . . well I think it's great you are so honest."

"I *think* I have a small penis too."

"Really?"

"Well, it's actually quite adequate, I've been told, only I think it's small. I'm sure compared to . . ."

"To . . . ?"

"Like black guys."

"Oh, don't you believe that myth. It's not at all true. Why my Sheldon ranked with the best of them."

After overcoming a momentary surge of jealousy, Jonathan becomes stiff. He now thinks about getting up to kiss her. There are no locks on these office doors by order of Dr. Leonard Warren but no one dares to come into the office during a session. There's an old couch in the room—it's small, covered with some kind of crummy green cloth, resting on tired wooden legs. Jonathan's never sat in it or used it and has wondered why it's even there. He's found himself, since this Beverly thing, thinking of himself and her on this couch, picturing her spread out on it, him on his knees, kissing up her leg.

Beverly sees something in his attitude that makes her cautious now. Things are moving a little fast. It's fairly obvious she has him but she doesn't know if she wants to reel him in yet.

"You know these sessions are beginning to feel less and less like therapy and more and more like . . ." Beverly says.

"I know." Silence. Then. "I don't know what to do about it," Jonathan says. "I tried to quit but that didn't work."

"Perhaps you should have."

Jonathan can't hide his painful reaction.

"No, not that it wouldn't disturb me deeply if you disappeared from my life . . . now . . . only I respect and understand the difficult position you are in."

"It's . . . extremely difficult . . . I . . ."

"Go on."

"I can't."

"I know."

"I want to . . ."

"I know I do too."

"You do?"

"Yes. But . . ."

Neither one of them has dared to gaze at the other during this hushed and hesitant conversation. Beverly is looking at a wall and Jonathan at a point on his desk.

"We have to talk this out," Jonathan says. "We mustn't . . . do anything."

"No, we mustn't."

"As long as we keep talking we can benefit from this entire experience. I'm talking about this with my own therapist."

"What does he say?"

"I don't think you want to know. I'm not sure I can explain it. He's crazy."

"You go to a crazy therapist?"

"Well, these days we have all kinds of therapists. Sometimes he thinks that crossing the line can lead to some kind of eventual fulfillment."

"Do you believe that too?"
"Sometimes I do. But it's scary."
Long pause.

Thaddeus and Morris Lieberman lean into the tape recorder.

"I'm going to leave now," Beverly says.
"Our time's not up."
"I have to go or . . ."
"Yes, it's . . . better . . ."

There's a sound of a chair being pushed back and then another one. Thaddeus and Morris Lieberman lean closer to the tape recorder, their earlobes nudging the black rectangular box as the tape slowly whirls.

After a few hours in The Expressway Motor Lodge right off the Van Wyck Expressway, Thaddeus went to Radio Shack and bought a bugging device which Luella installed with Thaddeus's help that very evening after office hours in Jonathan's phone, placing the tape recorder in her desk. After their heated primary encounter she brought out a legal agreement stating she's to get a quarter of any settlement or award arising out of any suit brought against the center by Thaddeus because of her assistance. She had worked for a lawyer before her job at the center so she's up on these things. Thaddeus readily signed.

Thaddeus and Morris Lieberman wait for the sound of the door being opened and closed. Nothing. They check the tape. It's still whirling. Then . . .
"Oh . . ." Beverly softly sighing.

Jonathan whispering something. They miss it. Then the door opens and closes.

"Shit!" Jonathan exclaims.

"Rewind!" Morris Lieberman demands. Thaddeus rewinds and turns the volume to maximum.

"You're so beautiful . . ." Jonathan whispers.

It's over. They stare at the tape. "Well?" Thaddeus asks. "Shit did he kiss her?"

"I don't know."

"Well?"

Morris cogitates. "Not good enough," he says.

"All that damn love talk?!"

"What love talk?"

"Let me tell you about my small penis! Let me tell you how fast I come. That's the Jewboy love-call! Flowers and violins to a woman like Beverly!"

"Where's the touching?" Morris exclaims. "There's no evidence of a touch."

"At the door?"

"We don't know what happened at the door. There's no hard, if you'll excuse the expression, evidence on that tape. These days therapists can get away with all that self-revelation as part of their technique. We don't have a case. We need a hand on a tit, an unsnapped bra, a finger up the cunt, a blow job . . . even a tongue kiss'll do. My friend, we don't have it. Yet."

Maureen is sitting in the park with Donna. Donna's been telling Maureen about the latest development in her affair with the Colonel. He's suddenly said he loves her and wants to get a divorce and marry her.

"The son of a bitch has put a big fright into me," Donna tells Maureen.

"Why? I thought you . . ."

"I do. I really do. But I don't know if I'm ready to take on the world. Do you know Italian families when it comes to this kind of thing?"

"Yeah, I think they're similar to Irish families."

"No, the Italians kill while the Irish just get into a drunken fistfight where no one really gets hurt—like that old movie *The Quiet One*. They never should have given these people equal rights until they cured everyone of prejudice. My family's the Ku Klux Klan of Howard Beach. A bunch of crazy, pill-popping guineas who'd put on a white sheet in a minute if they could find one that's not dirty. It's my luck to come from a family like this and then I have a thing with one of the biggest, blackest, in your face motherfuckas on the planet. Nothing light-skinned and polite about him. But what can I do? Even white girls have a little of the jungle in them. And now I got to make a decision. I mean for me to fool around, as long as nobody outside the office knows about it. I don't give a damn about the office because all the other girls are into it as well. It was fun until I started getting feelings and then when he started to drift away I was hurt and all but I was getting over it and I'd have been fine pretty soon. But for him to call me into his office this morning and give me all that love and marriage stuff. It freaks me out—even though it makes me happy too. I don't know what to do. Oh, Jesus, here comes your problem now."

"It's not a problem," Maureen says, looking over her shoulder to see a charging Thaddeus moving into the park. "Nothing significant is going on."

"I started with nothing significant too," Donna said. "After a while a girl wants a little . . . significance."

"Don't you dare go and leave me alone with him."

Thaddeus glowers, hovers over the bench as the girls sit and observe the ducks.

"Don't you have somewhere to go, girl?" Thaddeus asks Donna.

"I'm digesting my lunch," Donna answers.

"Walking digests it better."

"We all have different systems, Mr. Carmichael."

Thaddeus sits, wedging himself rudely between them. "I got to talk to you, girl." His back to Donna—too hot to keep any secrets now.

"Well talk . . ." Maureen says, peering around, afraid of Thaddeus causing embarrassment.

"My marriage is coming apart," Thaddeus says. "My damn wife wants to get it on with my marriage counselor. And he wants to get it on with her."

"What!?" Both girls exclaim in unison.

Maureen pictures the guy she saw quite briefly peering through the car window. Young, curly brown hair—not bad looking. She's seen Beverly at an office picnic and was deeply impressed with her beauty. One of the things that attracts her to Thaddeus is the beauty of his wife. She's always viewed a guy having a pretty girlfriend as a challenge.

"He's not supposed to do that kind of thing," Donna says. "He's supposed to be like a priest . . . only with boys."

"I want him to."

"What?!!" Both girls.

"Sue that motherfucking center for millions of dollars malpractice. I won't have to go out and sell me one more policy in my whole motherfucking life."

"That is despicable!" Maureen says.

"Listen, I got to go," Donna says.

"No, you stay." Maureen puts her hand on Donna's arm.

"Let her go. I got to talk to you. Alone."

Maureen lets Donna go.

"What are *we* going to do?" Thaddeus asks.

"*We?*"

"Yes, *we.*"

"There is no *we*. *We* is too complicated. I like simple. Right now it's *I. Me. You.* Okay. You got a kid. We're finished, you and me, before *we* even start."

"Listen, girl, I have no marriage and I'm on the brink of being rich. *We* move into New York City into one of those weird neighborhoods like Greenwich Village where they don't care who lives with who—they got boys with boys . . . girls with girls . . . they got slant-eyed Chinamen with big-lipped Africans . . . they got boys used to be girls and girls used to be boys. Shit a couple like *us* would be considered bourgeoisie down there. We don't have to get married right off—live together like hip people do these days. Maybe get out of the insurance business and do something finer. I want to become a landscape architect. And then I promote myself with wealthy people and before long I start making it big. Girl, you be the first to snag you a rich nigger. You be the envy of all the micks on your bar-studded block."

"Is this how you propose to a girl?"

"Propose?"

"Aren't you proposing?"

"Not marriage."

"No, not marriage, but cohabitation, isn't that right?"

"Yeah, I guess."

"A girl likes to hear more endearing things than how about being the first on your beer-soaked block to snag yourself a rich nigger or how would you like to move into a neighborhood of misfits, queers, and transsexuals. Do you think I stay up and worry about how I can be the envy of all my alcoholic friends by snagging me the first rich nigger who comes my way?"

"Well, I mean shit, girl, it stands to reason I lo . . ."

"Don't say it." Maureen stands up. "Don't say something desperate. Please."

Maureen moves out of the park in a determined way. Thaddeus almost starts after her so he can push her into the copse and maybe change her mind with some caresses but thinks better of it. He slumps. The black park attendant moves by picking up some paper with his pointed stick.

"Hey, man," Thaddeus says in a tired, friendly way. "How you doin'?"

"Doin' okay."

Yeah, happy ol' guy I bet. Going out on a pension pretty soon. His wife and a couple of kids probably grown and married, now maybe a grandpa. Grew up in an age where he didn't have to prove very much because nobody gave him a chance. You can't prove how good you can fight if they don't let you in the ring. Lucky ol' motherfucka really. Wouldn't mind trading places with him sometimes—yeah maybe now.

Thaddeus wearily leaves the park.

When Beverly gets home, Janelle is there with her mother, Audrey. Audrey knows Beverly is seeing a marriage counselor and views it as a waste of time but at least an important first step in getting rid of that loudmouthed son-in-law of hers. Her daughter doesn't appreciate that it's easier to get rid of a man in America than in Jamaica. Beverly has a degree in hotel management and could get a very good position—plus with her looks, get a much better man than this loudmouth. She has never gotten over the shock of her daughter getting pregnant by and then marrying this damn darky fool. She recalls with longing the white, Jewish ex-boyfriend even though he always looked dirty and was forever high on *ganja*. The worst thing that ever happened to her daughter was getting dumped, not by the guy, but by the guy's parents. Audrey regrets not being powerful enough with her daughter to dump Thaddeus. She did try but Beverly wouldn't listen. Audrey's worst fear had been that Beverly's baby would be coal black and would keep everyone awake at night with loudmouthed screaming. But thank God Janelle was as light-skinned as her mother and just as softly beautiful.

"How'd it go today?" Audrey asks.

"I don't know," Beverly replies. She peers around her small house. Hand-me-down living room furniture amidst new drapes and a beautiful dining room set with brand new, real china dishes in the hutch—the products of her overspending. It's depressing.

"You don't know?" Audrey presses on.

"We're going through some things . . ."

"Like?"

"Mother, we're not supposed to tell other people about what goes on in these sessions."

"I'm other people?"

"No, I don't mean it that way."

"I'm here supporting you 100 percent and I have a right to know what is happening. That man is no good."

Which man? Beverly wonders for the briefest wisp of time. Oh, her husband . . .

"I really don't think you ought to keep putting him down that way," Beverly says quietly, "Especially . . ."

She surreptitiously indicates Janelle. Audrey has never had a problem putting down her own husband in front of the children and until now Beverly has never stopped her from putting down Thaddeus in front of Janelle. But now Beverly has a new feeling about Thaddeus she hasn't digested yet. He fought to continue the marriage counseling. He gained insight. The old Thaddeus would have been delighted when Jonathan announced he was leaving but he was upset. Amazing.

"I want to talk to you," Thaddeus says to Beverly later in the afternoon when Janelle's taking a nap.

"Okay."

"What do you think is going on with our marriage counselor?"

"What do you mean?"

"You know what I mean."

"No, I don't."

"You blind? You want to get out of this rat hole and move to Long Island you better know."

"What are you talking about?"

"You got to get that man to move on you."

"What?!"

"You heard me. He moves on you and I sue that center for millions of dollars."

"I'm not going to do no such thing. I ain't no damn whore."

"Who says you have to be a whore?"

"Now I see why you didn't want him to quit. For a minute I thought you were really into getting some self-knowledge but I was wrong. You are scheming."

"I think this self-knowledge shit is just fine. You know what, though, you can buy you these Park Avenue long-bearded shrinks that stay with you till the day you die with a million dollar settlement—get you a Viennese wise man with a dead dick. Don't have to settle for no apprentice with a wandering eye. You can't get no real enlightenment with a young shrink got his hand up your skirt."

"You're crazy."

"Maybe he's afraid to do shit in that office. Too many eyes there. You got to get him to take you to a hotel. You got to get him to sign a register. I don't care if it's Mr. and Mrs. Schwartz—it's his handwriting. Subpoena that register and we got our case. You were led there by your counselor for a 'special' session, you thought, you got up in that room and oh, my god, he tried to . . ."

"And once I'm in the room with him?"

"Then do what you want. You want to fuck him you can. You don't want to fuck him you can do that too. Whatever you do you have to have a lot of remorse afterward. He clouded your mind. He made you do . . . whatever . . . all under the guise of therapy—quoting Freud with every motherfucking thrust. Your tears are copious. He has messed up your psyche, caused you irreparable psychological harm. How can you be a good mother and a good wife after what he has done to you? And he has deprived me of your wifely services. We came to him to repair our family and he has wrecked it instead."

Beverly is amused. He is deadly serious. He's been pondering and plotting this from the get-go. What a fool he is.

"You would let another man do that to your own wife?" she asks.

"It's for our daughter's future. You don't have to do shit if you don't want to. You don't have to tell me shit. I'll get over any jealousy once I'm sipping my champagne overlooking our beautiful green lawn in say, Syosset, or if the settlement is really good who knows . . . maybe Great Neck. Good school system there, Janelle grows up healthy and strong along with all the white kids of all those stockbrokers and captains of industry instead of here in Saint Albans with all the dope heads and winos. Well, what do you think?"

"I think you are crazy."

She leaves the room and starts to tidy up the kitchen while Thaddeus just lies around. He is ridiculous. But then she imagines Janelle growing up with decent people—yeah, white people. It wouldn't take much. Jonathan almost kissed her. It would be so easy. But she likes him and she'd have to betray him and she doesn't know if she could do that. Then she begins to wonder if she really more than likes him. She knows he's in love with her and now she begins to wonder if she's in love with him also. The idea scares her. It's Thaddeus's fault for even suggesting this kind of thing, putting the idea into her mind, changing a harmless flirtation attached to a real search for self-enlightenment into the possibility that she could really fall for Jonathan. And if she did fall for him and something did happen, what chance would she have? Those people of his are probably replicas of Sheldon's people.

She wouldn't stand a chance. She couldn't go through that again.

But maybe not. She doesn't know for sure, does she?

Beverly moves into the living room. "Why the hell don't we just get a divorce and be done with it?" she says. "You can't value me if you want me to do that with another man. I want a divorce!"

Thaddeus pays her no mind. He moves out of the room, goes upstairs, and dials his office, gets Donna at the switchboard, disguises his voice in case Maureen has told Donna she doesn't want to talk to him, and asks for Maureen.

"I got to talk to you, girl," he says when she comes on the line.

Maureen has spent most of the afternoon in and out of the ladies room in tears. She feels she's been unfair but mostly she's afraid her severe rhetoric will work. Damn, she's allowed herself to feel more strongly about Thaddeus than she wants. She really needs to get over it but maybe she doesn't want to.

"I'm sorry I was so harsh to you before," Maureen says. "I've been feeling really bad about it."

Beverly follows Thaddeus to pursue the argument and hears him disguise his voice. She moves into the bedroom and picks up the phone to listen. Thaddeus hears the click, knows it's Beverly, yet he goes on anyway. Fuckit.

"I got to see you, girl. We got to talk things out."

"All right," Maureen says. "Pick me up after work."

Thaddeus hangs up and waits. He leans back in the armchair. Beverly moves into the room. Thaddeus puts his hands in back of his head in imitation of Jonathan. Beverly leans against the wall and gazes at Thaddeus's now smug look.

"Sounds like a white girl," she says.

"Yeah . . ."

"One of the girls in the office?"

"You jealous?"

"You're still my husband, aren't you?"

Thaddeus smirks. "I guess."

The sun coming through the curtain illuminates Beverly's light-brown skin. Thaddeus looks at her in a fresh way—the way Jonathan looks at her. He feels a transcendent stirring. He is now Jonathan freshly peering at this unexplored fountain of sensuality. Beverly feels her skin tingle as Thaddeus slowly rises from his chair and moves to her. He is slow—casually intense. She feels like some other woman, perhaps the girl in the office—she's gone through all the possibilities and has concluded it must be the Irish girl, Maureen, because at the last office picnic she was the only one who didn't come near Thaddeus, at least while she was around. Beverly liked the way Maureen looked, buxom, typically Irish with understanding, sympathetic eyes. Yeah, the voice matched too. Maureen. Thaddeus is crazy about her. And he wants me to know. Well, yes, I do know and . . . now Thaddeus is moving toward me in a different way—not like a pig in the barnyard but like a real lover who knows what he is doing with a woman. All at once she feels as if she's Maureen and she's receptive to this man who now is moving forward to kiss her.

They kiss softly, the "wronged husband," the "wronged wife"—a topsy-turvy feeling, strangely exhilarating. In each other's arms, touching and feeling; it's as if they'd never done that before. They lose all sense of the past. There is only her lovely skin and bountiful breasts for Thaddeus as he slips off Beverly's blouse and bra, and for Beverly there are only his delicate fingers on her body, velvet strokes and loving kisses all over her face, worshipped by devouring eyes. And then they are together on the couch and Thaddeus has put his lips to her vagina and she blocks the resentment because he has never done that before. She has a most unexpected orgasm. And then she worships at his cock with her mouth, something she's only done in a perfunctory way, wishing she could swallow it and make it part of her. She suddenly turns and makes him enter from behind because it penetrates the most deeply that way and she has another orgasm. Thaddeus is kissing her back and neck, then they stand and face each other daring the other to not break the spell. No Jamaican this or black American that—no credit card problems, no staying out late, no Jonathan Meltzer and no Maureen—nothing but twenty-ish, firm flesh, man-woman. They meld and Beverly lies on the couch, spreads herself, and takes Thaddeus into her. He is handsome. I really always thought so . . . that's really why I started with him to begin with. He has nice eyes and strong, masculine features. She comes again. The vibrations of her cunt reverberate all through him. No one has ever fucked him like this before.

"I love you," he says.

"I love you," she says.

And then they explode together.

Chapter Eight

Timothy's jaw drops like an old biddy listening to outrageous gossip as Jonathan starts talking before his ass even hits the seat.

"I know you're going to think I've gone absolutely bananas and maybe I have but so what?! You believe in all that, don't you? Insanity is a sane reaction to an insane world? Breaking down barriers. Well, you're right. I never really thought so before. I first came to you because you were hip, eclectic, a little wild and unpredictable—all the kids loved you—the flavor of the month. But I was always basically a nice Jewish boy from Merrick, Long Island, toying with this shit as a way of being edgy until now I'm really edgy."

"Would you mind telling me what you are talking about?" Timothy asks. He's been kicking himself for spilling his guts out about the baseball player. He ought to maybe have a few sessions with a conventional shrink if he can find one he respects. This self-revealing therapy can sometimes be, well . . . too self-revealing. He's afraid of what he might have unleashed in Jonathan. Sure, Jonathan's basically a nice kid with nothing really bizarre in his makeup but you never can tell what kind of crazy shit a guy like him can get into. And now the wide eyes, the frantic speech, the wildly beseeching look. Timothy can hardly pay attention to what Jonathan is raving about because he feels so guilty. But now he better concentrate to find out what upheaval he's caused so he tunes in and asks a pertinent question.

"Would you mind telling me, in a somewhat linear way, what is going on?" Timothy asks.

Timothy is continually disappointing Jonathan. God, doesn't he know? Hasn't he been paying attention?

"I don't know how to say this," Jonathan says. "I don't want it to sound too grandiose like 'the love of my life' or too trivial like 'oh what a beautiful dish.' I don't want to describe my feelings with a string of clichés like sleepless nights or surging violins."

"You and . . . ?"

"Yes."

"What's her name?"

"Beverly . . . God, like I was afraid just now to tell you as if you were the school principal asking about some partner in a prank and I ratted on her and she would get in trouble."

"Then you feel you're doing something wrong?"

"Yes, yes, yes, of course yes. The feeling of something wrong is our Montague and Capulet. Can't you see that?! I have found my soul mate! Oh, sure it's wrong. She's a client but she's also a radiant, lovely human being who was made to be my love. You've got to help me. Don't waste my time trying to talk me out of her. I love her."

"Okay, what would you like to do?"

"Well, for one thing cure my premature ejaculation."

"How much time do I have?"

"I also have a small-penis complex."

Jonathan had taken a physical exam before starting treatment as part of the standard operating procedure but the report never said a thing about a stunted cock. Of course a standard medical exam really doesn't get into measuring a guy's cock, yet, upon reflection, an exam that precedes a male's psychotherapy certainly should examine the phallus because much of therapy basically revolves around it. It's like yeah I feel my cock is too small and indeed it turns out to be all of two tiny inches so where's the neurosis?

Yet Timothy could foresee problems in calling a guy's doctor to ask for a phallus measurement as part of a physical exam. He'd better discuss it at the next shrink convention to see if he can get the ball rolling. Actually it's a rather brilliant idea and if it gets anywhere his name might get attached to it. A physical exam with a Mitchell Measurement.

"Is your penis small?" Timothy asks.

Oh, God, he's not going to ask to see it, is he?

"No, it's not really small. I'm quite normal. I mean I sneak looks at other guys in locker rooms and stuff. They're about the same as me." He recalls that black monstrosity he saw shoved into that white girl's mouth by Thaddeus. It looked like an ebony baseball bat.

Jonathan measures his dick before every date hoping against rational hope for an improvement. He also sticks a six-inch ruler deeply into the base of his cock after he gets a hard-on before jerking off. The helmet head of his dick barely misses the five-inch mark. He shoves it deeper till it hurts and makes the five inches. He enviously gazes at the inch that mockingly protrudes over the head of his dick. He wishes there was an exercise that could build up his cock, like a bulking up for the arms and chest. He would even settle for wider if he couldn't get longer. He once jokingly asked a medical student and the guy told him the cock couldn't be bulked up.

"I told her about my problems," Jonathan says. "She understood."

"You told . . . uh . . . ?" Timothy asks.

"Beverly."

"Yes, I remembered her name, you told Beverly about your small penis?"

"No, my feeling that it's small."

"About premature ejaculation too?"

"Yes."

"How about flatulence problems or allergies? Get into that?"

"What are you driving at?"

"Seems to me an amazing choice of topics preceding a hoped-for romantic liaison, don't you think?"

"I shouldn't have done that?"

"I'm not passing judgment, all I'm saying is it's unusual, I think that's fair to say, don't you?"

"Yes." Jonathan is instantly depressed. He's fucked up. Of course you don't tell a woman that. What woman wants to be made love to by a guy who comes in a second and has a small dick?

"Are you all right?" Timothy asks as he watches Jonathan turn pale and pasty.

"No."

"Um-huh."

"What do I do now?"

"About?"

"Her."

"I think it might be valuable for us to explore why you told her what you told her."

"All right, I wanted to be honest with her."

"Why?"

"Because I love her."

"Um-huh, are we always honest with the ones we love?"

"We should be, but she's so overwhelmingly beautiful that I didn't want to disappoint her. It's like what does a creature like that see in me? I wanted her to know about my inadequacies rather than her finding out for herself. I didn't want her to . . ."

"Go on . . ."

"Laugh at me?"

"Have you been laughed at before?"

"Not by girls."

"By who?"

"My mother. She caught me with a hard-on in the bath when I was like twelve or thirteen, just before my bar mitzvah and she laughed at my little 'schmekel.' She said 'Maybe when you're bar mitzvah you'll have a manly one.' I could have drowned myself in the bathtub. It really never grew bigger. I mean it's virtually the same. I have a small cock."

Jonathan starts to cry. Timothy moves the box of tissues closer to him and Jonathan takes one and wipes his eyes.

"I worry about that so much every time I go to bed with a girl—especially the first time. So I always kind of go with girls who really aren't that much into sex—you know, Jewish girls. A fuck to them is like a step toward something official like an engagement or marriage. These days even Jewish girls have to fuck before marriage but they can't obliterate centuries of genetic frigidity so to them a guy can't come fast enough and there's no such thing as a small cock. But Beverly is a black woman! A fucking beautiful savage! I know she's had plenty of lovers before marriage and possibly even during marriage—if her husband can be believed. Black girls didn't have to wait for any sexual revolution to love fucking these black guys with *schvances* like horses!"

"I wouldn't worry about premature ejaculation or small penis anxiety at this point," Timothy says. "Why don't you try to figure out how the whole thing came to this? Has anything happened yet?"

"No, almost but not quite. I've decided I'm going to go for it."

"Are you still going to treat them as a couple?"

"Yes, I can't escape. I tried but failed. I think I want to marry her."

"Does she have any children?"

"Yes, a two-year-old daughter. Janelle."

"Going to raise her too?"

"Yes."

"You're trying to ennoble a hard-on. Wars have been fought because of that—think of Helen of Troy. Why can't you just fuck her and let it go? Why all this marriage and raising someone else's kid all of a sudden? Are you so fucking guilt-ridden that the only way to justify it is with this love of my life bullshit? Give the girl as good a screw as possible in the second it takes you to come. When you come too fast the first time, fuck her again in like five minutes—you're a young guy . . . the second time you might last two minutes and then maybe twenty minutes later fuck her again and just keep fucking her all day. Don't worry about premature ejaculation. Use it. Tell the girl it's because she's so beautiful you couldn't help yourself. So stop feeling so guilty. I don't think you're going to fuck this woman up. She sounds as if she knows what she's doing and you wouldn't be the first therapist who's screwed his client. So do it. Don't get caught though. The neurosis is not in the act itself but in the sloppy cover-up of the act. I'd like to be able to talk you out of crossing the line but you seem too far gone.

"Now another thing. This is what you really pay me for. You're attempting to emulate a stereotypical black guy. A big dick. Fucks like crazy. Yeah man, life is tough for the black man except maybe on Saturday night. You're not accepting your own libido. You've replaced it with some of your client's. *You* want to fuck this girl? *You*, Jonathan Meltzer, well go ahead and do it but let it be *you* and if there are consequences *you* take them like a big boy and if there are no consequences, no compelling need to ennoble the relationship, then *you* have a ball.

"Fill me in on all the details next time. I love a good descriptive sex session. Oops our time is up."

Maureen waits for Thaddeus in her car in the office parking lot but he doesn't show. After a half hour she pulls out of the lot and heads east along Hillside Avenue for her home in Rosedale. Then at 181st Street she suddenly veers south and heads back west into the Saint Albans area. On one level she tells herself she's driving aimlessly because she's not ready to face the emptiness of home yet. On a deeper level she knows she wants to drive past Thaddeus's house. She does that whenever she gets interested in a guy. Her last serious guy, Tom, lived in Washington Heights and the night before they were to make love for the first time she drove up there, parked, and gazed at his apartment house—large, anonymous . . . meaningless really . . . except after she drove away Tom had more of a dimension for her. Her guys have to come from someplace—exist in some other way than in her own mind, in order for her to really allow herself to get into them. She's stunned because Thaddeus stood her up, not that she's mad or upset about it as a pride thing . . . but his doing it to her makes her more keenly interested in him. She was there for him and he knew it—and then he doesn't show. Wow. There *is* something special about the guy then.

She follows the street names until she finds the street where he lives. She checks the numbers on the detached houses with their little postage stamp pieces of land against the office roster she has by her side until she drives by his house. It's dark green, a small Cape Cod style house, no better or worse than any of its neighbors except it's well landscaped. There are signs of life within—a light in the upstairs window, the front door ajar, and the storm door closed. She drives by slowly, there's no parking until she gets to the corner. She parks opposite a small convenience store. Now she looks around. Four or five men standing around near the front of the store, a woman on the periphery of the group, some loud talk and laughter. Most of the guys look disheveled and a little drunk or maybe high. She needs a pack of cigarettes but does she want to get out and go to that store to get it? It's dusk now. She's aware of herself as a white girl in an all-black neighborhood. She can tell by the way some of the guys throw surreptitious glances her way that she's been noticed. She's afraid and would really like to pull away but then she finds herself wondering what it would feel like to simply get out of the car, all of her freckled, Irish, twenty-two-year-old self, in this neighborhood, a few doors down from the black man she's going to go to bed with, to simply buy a pack of cigarettes at that store. Would anyone accost her? What harm is she doing them? She suddenly moves out of the car and heads for the store. She can feel a subtle change in the group as they scrutinize everything about her. Her mouth is dry and she needs to control her steps so she doesn't speed up and appear panicky. She reaches the store and there are people milling around near the counter. A bearded man behind the counter is watching a small TV. She asks for a pack of Newport cigarettes in a scratchy, hardly audible voice. The store owner carefully lays the pack on the counter. She picks it up and hands him a bill and waits for change. The man says thank you. She replies you're welcome. When she moves out of the store there's a cop's car in front of hers. A pang of fear shoots through her. There's no one in front of the store now—the street's cleared. Inside the cop's car there's an Irish face peering out at her. Could it be her cousin Patrick? She'll tell him not to tell her mother or father. But then it's not Patrick.

"Is there anything wrong, miss?" the cop says. His name tag says Kennedy.

Maureen moves slowly to the car. "No, I just needed some cigarettes," she says, showing him the pack as evidence.

"It's not the best neighborhood to shop in especially when the sun goes down."

There's a black cop driving the police car. He leans over and says. "Where do you live, miss?"

"In Rosedale."

"You're a little out of your way, aren't you?" The black cop's voice is harsh, suspicious. The only white kids who come here are looking to score drugs.

"I just needed a pack of cigarettes."

"Is that your car?"

"Yeah, it's my car."

"Follow us. Farmers Boulevard right into the Belt. Take you right to Rosedale."

"I know the way. That's okay."

"Miss, I wouldn't get mixed up in this kind of thing if I was you," the Irish cop says.

"This kind of thing?" Maureen asks.

"I think you know."

She doesn't say anything.

"There are programs, miss," the black cop says. "We can give you a number to call."

"I'm okay. I don't do anything."

She moves away toward her car. They can't even fathom the idea that she might be there because of a guy—a black guy.

But then she gets mad at herself. These sons of bitches are getting my Irish up. Thaddeus is a man. He is not an inferior man because he's black. I've kissed him, made out with him. What kind of world is this?

She drives her car toward the Belt with the cops trailing politely behind her.

They hardly know what to say to each other. They assemble themselves and wordlessly go into separate rooms. They don't look at each other.

Beverly needs the introspective umbrella of a shower.

She tries to wash away a sinking, depressed feeling. She's confused. She desperately gropes for perspective. She needs to see Jonathan but how can she tell him about what just happened?

Thaddeus puts on his gardening clothes and goes outside to check out his vegetable garden in the back of the house. He's there as Maureen drives by. If she'd seen him on his knees in old dungarees, pulling a weed, putting in some plant food, she'd have been impressed—a side of him she never would have suspected yet wouldn't have been surprised to find. Beverly hates this nature-loving side of Thaddeus though she has no objection to pretty flora and fauna. To her it's simply another way Thaddeus has of escaping her and her needs. Thaddeus can become more fully enmeshed in the fate and future of his plants than anything else, except maybe his daughter.

He greets his next-door neighbor Clyde Simpkins. He's just sold him a mortgage insurance policy and he's trying to convert it to a more ambitious whole life. Simpkins says maybe . . . he'll talk to the wife about it. Thaddeus digs out some weeds. His life is like the fertile soil beneath his feet. Rich and abundant—only he needs to pull weeds . . .

There's something new about Thaddeus that allows Clyde Simpkins to invite him to come to church this Sunday. They've got a guest preacher at the South Jamaica Baptist Church who's supposed to be inspiring. Thaddeus's mother is a churchwoman and Thaddeus always gets the heebie-jeebies with that whole damn scene. But now he surprises himself by saying he might come and maybe meaning it. He enjoys the big, warm smile on Simpkins's face when he says that. Will getting involved with the church be good for business? But then he casts that avaricious thought out of his mind—like Jesus casting out the moneymen from the temple. Getting involved with the church might be good for his soul and his soul should be his main business.

He's tired of the rat race that is the damn insurance business—sell, sell, sell every moment, not one pure thought, go to church because it might be good for business. Say hello to this one and be nice to that one because there might be a sale in it. Why can't his life be peaceful and full of love? Simpkins makes a steady salary, has two nice kids and a pretty good wife—a big, peaceful-looking man with a nice word for everyone. Thaddeus thinks about the park attendant in that little park where . . . then he remembers about Maureen. He was supposed to meet her. He stood her up. She'll be pissed.

So what? He doesn't need her anymore. He's got a wife who loves him. Still, having two women is better than one, isn't it?

No. There he is a greedy, grubby life insurance peddler wanting to gobble up everything in sight like some damn pig. Irish girl giving him lectures about being a black man. He doesn't need that. He is a black man in a white man's world but so is Simpkins and look how happy he is. And look how happy I am now—now I know my wife loves me and I love her and we've tapped into a love that still burns hot. Got nothing to do with black, white anything else like that.

He finishes up his gardening in a relaxed, casual way. Some plants doing okay over here and some not so well over there. That's what it's all about. You just have to understand it. He moves into the house and goes upstairs. Beverly is changing Janelle's clothes in the bedroom. He stays in the frame of the door and peers at his wife and daughter, tries to catch Beverly's eye but Beverly's not allowing that to happen. Okay, he sits on the bed and puts Janelle on his lap while Beverly is tying the child's shoes. Again tries to catch her eye. She's not looking at him. He wants to say something but words catch in his throat because there are no words for what he wants to say. Beverly picks up Janelle and moves downstairs to give Janelle her supper. She hasn't looked at Thaddeus once since it happened.

It's bedtime. He's her husband, right. But what is he expecting of her now?

Thaddeus, in pj's, slides between the sheets and picks up his well-worn copy of *Think and Grow Rich* by Napoleon Hill but now there's something slightly repellent about that classic sales tome. He puts it down. He's been given a paperback of essays by an Indian philosopher named Krishnamurti that a lot of the Jewish guys in the office are reading. The picture of the man on the cover conveys a sense of simple human warmth and wisdom—the profile of an older man, probably not very tall, partially bald, with kind yet fiercely intelligent eyes. He starts to read, waiting for the guy to preach some sort of love everyone stuff but he's immediately disarmed because Krishnamurti appeals to an intelligent kind of emotionality that is revolutionary to Thaddeus. There's no clarion call to love thy neighbor as thyself which, if followed, will lead to immediate success and the five million dollar round table. There's only a method of viewing life experience that is at once simple, startlingly deep, yet surprisingly quite accessible. All the materialism Thaddeus has come to believe to be at his very core is undermined almost from the first paragraph yet there's no romance of poverty here, no rush to shed your riches. To Krishnamurti that kind of thing is irrelevant—one can do quite well in the world and still view life through the prism of a sublime kind of intelligence that one needn't journey to the mountains of Tibet to attain.

Beverly moves into the bedroom, slips her most modest dressing gown out of the closet, and dresses for bed in the bathroom. Though she doesn't need them, she puts curlers in her hair and rubs her skin with Noxzema, an odor guaranteed to turn off the most lustful satyr. Then she moves out and slips into her side of the bed, turns her back, and audibly yawns. Thaddeus, aware of his wife in bed with him, reflects that though she's been distant and even standoffish since *it* happened it's not anything to worry about—a feminine thing. His constant sense of impatience is blunted. Rome wasn't built in a day. She's been shocked about what happened and she can't talk about it. That's okay. He understands. Krishnamurti writes about the burdens we put on others by expectations, which have nothing to do with them and quite often even have nothing to do with what we really want ourselves. Life is a constant flow of false expectations, promises never really made yet still perceived as broken.

Beverly lies there and begins to fume. For the first time since *it* happened she thinks about that Irish girl angrily. This joker here in bed with me now feels he's got it made, doesn't he? He's got his Irish girlfriend and now his wife. He must think he's some sort of a goddamn oil sheik in Saudi Arabia!

She sits up in bed and glares at Thaddeus pretending to be absorbed in one of his stupid inspirational sales books.

"What's her name?" she asks.

"Who?"

"That girl."

"Oh, her . . . Maureen."

"Was she good?"

"Good?"

"In bed?"

"We never went to bed."

"Oh?"

"Not yet. I wanted to."

"You did?"

"Yes, but not anymore. Things are going to be different now. I'm going to be different."

"Okay, then you admit . . ."

"Admit what?"

"About what you've done in the past. Staying out all hours . . . all that."

"You only want me to say something so you can use it to block your new feelings about me. You're afraid of them." This with an air of sagacity. Beverly stares at him in amazement.

"You can go to sleep now," he says. "I know how you feel. It's all right. You have no obligation. We burden ourselves by useless tasks rather than allowing our simple, pure emotions to flow like a stream from our brain, our hearts, and our unconscious mind."

Beverly is relatively certain Thaddeus doesn't do drugs in any kind of serious way. They've both done pot together but he hasn't been doing it or she'd have whiffed it. He might have taken something psychedelic though. Sometimes Sheldon, on some weird stuff, would get philosophical too but then he'd giggle and turn red. Thaddeus is exhibiting no physical symptoms of drug use. She goes to sleep. Thaddeus finishes a large section of the Krishnamurti, puts it down and cuddles into his wife's back, and snuggles his arm around her.

Beverly dreams a boa constrictor has wrapped itself around her and is crushing her.

When Beverly wakes in the morning, Thaddeus is not in bed with her. He's gotten up early and gone out. She's grateful he's not around. She calls information and asks for Meltzer in Merrick, Long Island. There are two Meltzers listed there, none by the name of Jonathan. She stares at the names attempting to divine which might be his.

Dr. Simon Meltzer, 3148 Lakeland Drive, or Rebecca Meltzer, 14 Janus Lane.

Is Jonathan's father a doctor? Seems logical. Jonathan going for his doctorate—his father a doctor. What kind of doctor? Maybe a surgeon. They do very well. And they're educated too—not those grubby business types like Sheldon's parents who never even went to college. She starts to dial the doctor's phone number but becomes nervous and instead decides to do the one it's least likely to be, as a way of practice. The phone rings twice before it's picked up.

"Yes, who is it?"

Beverly hates the rasping, rough female voice.

"Is Mr. Jonathan Meltzer home?"

"Who is this?"

"My name is Mrs. Carmichael. I am a client of his, from the Jamaica Family Center."

"Oh?" Rebecca Meltzer is immediately suspicious. She doesn't like the voice because it's an island *schvatza* voice. What's a client doing calling Jonathan's home? She doesn't like this kind of intrusion. Let him deal with all the lowlifes in Jamaica there—why bring all that *drek* out here.

"I'll see if he's in."

Jonathan's mother calls him to the phone and lingers to see if she can pick up any of the conversation.

"Hello," Jonathan says.

"Hi, it's . . ."

"Oh, hi . . ."

"I'm sorry to be calling you at . . ."

"No, that's okay."

"I'd like to see you."

"Well, I can give you an appointment tomorrow. I'm not at the center today."

"No, I'd like to see you today, away from the center."

"Oh . . ."

"It's very important."

"Has something happened?"

"Yes, in a way . . . I don't know . . . please. It's hard to explain on the phone."

"Can you come to New York? I have classes all day. Can we meet in Washington Square Park?"

"Yes."

"Say at noontime?"

"I'll be there by the fountain."

They hang up.

Rebecca catches Murray coming down the stairs.

"Who was that?" Murray asks.

"For Jonathan." She puts her hand on his arm. Murray shakes it off. "I'm in a hurry," he says petulantly.

"I didn't like this phone call to Jonathan," she says. "It was a woman, sounded like maybe from Jamaica or someplace like that . . . said she was a client of his from that center."

"So?"

"He's been strange lately. Something on his mind."

"Listen, I'm late for an appointment."

"You find out what's happening with your son." The order is issued.

Jonathan's not going to meet Beverly. All he needs right now, at the onset of a promising career, is to be mixed up in a mess. All the years of study down the drain. And he's going to change his crazy therapist too. The guy's out of his mind. I need someone to tell me not to do it and instead I get this fuck her with your own libido shit! For this kind of advice I have to see a shrink? I could get that in a bar—an unusually erudite bar, admittedly, but a bar nevertheless.

He's decided to masturbate over her. Do that until the entire situation resolves itself. You can't go to jail for who you jerk off on.

"So how's it going?" his father asks as they walk to the garage.

"Yeah, okay."

"Still seeing that girl, Arlene?"

"Yeah, more or less."

"Are we going to meet her?"

"Well, I don't know if I'm ready for that yet."

"How's it going at this Jamaica Center?"

"Oh, interesting."

"What do you do there? Like drug counseling?"

"Well, some of that, some individual psychotherapy, some marriage counseling. Good experience for me."

"Yeah, I bet you run into some crazy things down there."

"Well, no more than anywhere else. People are people."

"Oh, sure, but down there you don't get the same kinds of things you'd get say if you had a counseling job in Merrick or Baldwin or Oceanside. There you get the welfare, the alcoholism, the abandoned and abused kids in the worst poverty. Pitiable, my heart goes out to those people."

They are about to get to the garage.

"What do you get here, Dad?" Jonathan asks.

"Here?"

"Yeah, here, Merrick, Baldwin, Oceanside, what do we get here?"

"What do you mean?"

"Nothing," he shrugs. He stops himself for lacing into his father about the boring, duplicitous life he's chosen for himself. Sure, makes a nice living, nice house, great kids—everything *copacetic*, right, Dad?

If that's so then why do you still have a Dominican girlfriend, a bookkeeper from one of your accounts? Everyone in the family knows about her, including your own wife, because you wanted to get a divorce and marry this woman five years ago and mom wouldn't hear of it and instead she said, my own mother, that you can do whatever you want as long as you don't break up the family and you went along with it—just great, except from there on in you developed a mean set of ulcers, your weight is getting out of control, your secret drinking's not all that secret, and you look like you're a prime candidate for a heart attack at the early age of fifty-five.

And my mom, never an easy woman, has become a thoroughly bitter woman.

So how did Jonathan and the whole family know about this? His mother made sure to have big, loud hysterical fights so that the whole family could hear as a way of shaming his father into not taking the action he wanted to.

All this out here on the South Shore of Long Island. Nice houses, nice family. Make a living, send the kids to college, then retire to sunny Florida and die a fulfilled person.

And him? If he's married to Arlene, two or three kids down the line, along would come a Beverly and he'd fall madly in love and have to make a choice, so what would he do? Like his father? And Arlene like his mother? It makes his heart sick, but he's probably going to do it anyway. Last night, before she started all that homosexual bullshit, he almost asked Arlene to get engaged.

He's at the brink of his entire life but he knows he can't risk what will happen to him if he goes further with Beverly. He can't do it.

They're at the garage.

"Listen, you're not . . . fooling around down there, are you?" his dad asks.

"No, it wouldn't pay."

"Yeah," his dad says. An entire wasted life in that "yeah." A beat man. It's a devil's bargain his father made with his mother and it's going to kill them both. Maybe that'll be okay too because they're not living all that well anyway.

They've never had one close communication with each other—never once. Jonathan's dad holds his hand out to Jonathan and they shake. There's something he's trying to convey to his son with a very strong handshake. Jonathan's father sees hope in his son's youth and promise. He squeezes Jonathan's hand hard, begging his son to escape something he can't even define himself. Jonathan winces. He turns away quickly and scampers to the car. Jonathan's father watches his son depart, checks his watch, and rushes not to be late for his appointment. Maybe afterward he can stop off and get a drink.

Jonathan calls Beverly on his cell. He's been endlessly going over what he's going to say to her. This is the best he's come up with:

"Listen, I think we have to take a step back and look at this objectively. After all, one can't go through life simply acting on strong impulses. There's a great deal at stake here. I think it would be a mistake to meet outside the center."

But the thought of saying it makes him almost depressed. He imagines her hanging up on him and never seeing her again—her never coming back to the center. He's gotten too involved. Maybe he's going into the wrong field. Maybe he's not meant to be a therapist. He could switch to research once he obtains his doctorate though he's a little weak there. Or maybe he could see a real Freudian shrink—one needs to get them while they're still alive because they're dying off quickly. Then he could be a good therapist, which is what he wants to be because he really believes it's his calling. Meanwhile he's not able to make the call as he wends his way into Manhattan to attend morning classes. Maybe a call would not be the right thing. Maybe he simply ought to meet her and they could talk, there, face-to-face. No, he has to make himself call her. He has to do the right thing.

Chapter Nine

"I broke off with him," Donna tells Maureen on their break as they're walking outside the office. "I feel real good about it. Like a skyscraper off my back."

"What did he say when you told him?"

"He said okay. I think he was relieved too." Actually Donna feels like shutting herself up in her room, crying endlessly, and never coming out. "It's no good. The whole damn thing. I'm never going to date a married guy again. You always get hurt."

"Is it just the married thing?" Maureen asks.

"No, not just that."

Maureen waits knowingly.

"Hey, I was brought up a certain way and even though it's wrong it's hard to change," Donna replies defensively. "I can't see me like married to a black guy, having a kid, and being deadly scared about the baby coming out dark with kinky hair and stuff even though sometimes I think these guys and some of the women are beautiful. Maybe somewhere along the line . . . maybe twenty, thirty, or a hundred years from now it won't make any difference but for now I can't do it. If I have all these problems within myself how am I going to stand up to my family when they start cursing me out and telling me about how they aren't going to want to have anything to do with any black kid of mine? It would kill me. It really would. You know, as much as I put 'em down as a bunch of grease balls, they're part of me and I can't erase that. Just like your background is part of you, Maureen. Maureen?"

"Yeah."

"You okay?"

"I don't know. I was supposed to see him last night. He stood me up. Made me a little crazy. I drove to his block, looked at his house. Cops came and figured I was trying to score some drugs and escorted me out of the neighborhood. That bothered me a lot. The way they treated me."

"What did they say?"

"They were polite, but I began to feel . . . like this is supposed to be America, right? If I was a black girl in that car they'd have passed me by, not even worried if I was there to buy drugs or not but because I'm white they worried."

"Yeah, so that's just the way it is."

"It really bothered me, it still does. One time I told him he's making too much of this race thing but now I don't know. If I was brought up the way he was maybe you really can't help making too much of it because it must be with you every second of the time."

They put out their cigarettes and head back to the office. Before they go in, Donna says, "Listen you're not going to be like no Joan of Arc or something, are you?"

"Joan of Arc?"

"Yeah, like a lady with a cause."

"They burned her at the stake, right?"

"Yeah, they fried her good."

Thaddeus owes Maureen an explanation. He can see he's hurt her and he's not going to hurt anyone anymore through insensitivity and anger. It's true some people bring hurt upon themselves, but Maureen's not one of them.

He calls her on the interoffice phone. "Listen, I think we ought to have a talk."

"What about, Mr. Carmichael?" Maureen asks coldly.

"I think you know what about. I think we need to resolve things."

"They're resolved, aren't they?"

"No, I think I owe you some sort of explanation."

"You don't owe me a thing, Mr. Carmichael. I'm sorry I'm busy now." Maureen hangs up, takes a break, moves into the ladies room where she bursts into tears. Donna knocks on Thaddeus's office door, opens it, and moves in.

"What the hell did you do to her?" Donna asks a startled Thaddeus. "She's like a basket case."

"I didn't do anything to her."

"You know you guys like to fuck around and you don't care about the consequences, do you? They let you in the candy store and you're attacking all the goodies and not giving a shit. Well, wise up, Mr. Carmichael, you can get hurt too you know just like you go around hurting someone else!"

Donna slams the door behind her.

Thaddeus waits for Maureen after work in the office parking lot in his car. She doesn't acknowledge him, gets in her car, and drives while he follows her. She wends her way to Ozone Park—the same lonely, dead-end street where they first made out—and waits for him. Thaddeus is put off by where she parks. It's dusk now and he almost feels she's setting a trap for him. He gazes around as if looking for white hoods that'll come out of the bushes and attack him. He's being silly so he moves out of his car and into hers.

"Look" he says. "I've been wrong. Wrong about a lot of things. I'm a married guy with a kid—I need to make some major changes in my life and I'm starting now. I'm going to devote myself to my family for one thing."

"Do you love her?" Maureen cuts in.

"Yeah, I think I do," Thaddeus says, not daring to look at Maureen. "Something happened yesterday that changed everything."

"What?"

"I . . . can't really tell you."

"Yes, you can," her voice hard. She has to know.

"It's hard to explain but I started to look at her with fresh eyes . . . maybe the way that therapist looks at her, and something happened with her too and we . . . got together like we never did before and then I started to look at the way I look at the world with fresh eyes too—my resentments, my bullshit—the things you told me about race and shit . . . the things I felt I needed to vindicate myself as a man. I'm making a fresh start in every way of my life. I want to leave the insurance business and get a degree in landscape architecture. There was a lady I got friendly with—not that way—when I sold her a car and that's what she did. I called her up and she remembered me and I told her I wanted to work for her while I studied . . . maybe at first just lugging plants around and digging holes or whatever but I want to learn. She said yeah great . . . can't pay me very much but she'll teach me as we go along."

"You're quitting the insurance business?"

"Yeah, it's just the worst thing in the world for a guy like me—reinforces every damn problem I ever had. Maybe things'll be a little tight financially at first, hell I'll max out my credit cards—whatever it takes. I got a good family—a beautiful wife, a beautiful kid—so why am I trying to jeopardize that. Do you understand what I'm saying to you?"

"All right," she says flatly. "What do you want from me?"

"I want you to understand."

"Why?"

"Because . . . I . . . care about you."

She lights a cigarette and opens the window so the smoke will blow out. They sit for a while saying nothing.

"I'm in love with you," she says. "It's okay. I've been in love before and I know how to get over it. I'm not telling you to put any pressure on you. In a way I'm glad you love your wife. I'm sure she's really a very nice person and it's good your getting out of the life insurance business. Funny, I always sensed you had some kind of artistic ability you never used. This way it's going to be a lot simpler for both of us to get on with our lives."

It's time for Thaddeus to go. He's made her understand but he can only sit as she idly smokes her cigarette.

"Maureen," he says looking directly at her for the first time. And they go at each other voraciously.

"Don't fuck with me now," she tells him as she slips off her panties, straddles him in the car seat, while he unbuckles his belt and pulls his pants down. "Just fuck me, motherfucka."

It didn't happen, Thaddeus tells himself as he drives home. It happened but it didn't happen. It was a carryover from the way I used to be, that's all. It was wrong. I made a mistake getting in a place like that with her. Shit, I'm still a man and too damn weak to turn away. I got to have will power, that's all it takes. From here on in it's will power.

Beverly dresses as stylishly as she can but when she step off the subway and wends her way to Washington Square Par she realizes she looks provincial—her makeup, hairstyle—a b old hat compared to these kids on this bright spring day. Sh been away a few years, got married, had a kid, bought a lit

house, marriage counseling, maybe a divorce in the works. She's changed.

The park's pretty much the same as it used to be when she hung out there with Sheldon except there's some construction going on at the south side. She recognizes a guitar player from the old days—a guy with long stringy black hair except now there are strands of grizzly gray. She moves around the park, half looking for Jonathan and half remembering all the times she spent here with Sheldon. At one point Sheldon rehearsed here with his group, attracting an admiring crowd, accepting donations and using it to immediately buy drugs.

It's past twelve and she sits on the rim of the dry, dirty fountain peering around for Jonathan, wondering if he'll come, wondering what she's going to say, wondering why she even needs to see him except she knows he will try to make her understand what she really wants.

Jonathan is behind a tree, watching her since she came into the park. She's perfectly made up; her lacquered hair so long it almost reaches the small of her back. Her jeans clinging as if pressed on, the peasant blouse with the slightest bit of cleavage all making her seem like a steaming torrent of sexuality planted in the middle of a park filled with grungy, mostly asexual kids and shuffling neighborhood freaks.

He moves out from behind the tree and walks hurriedly toward the fountain. She smiles broadly as she sees him approach.

"I'm sorry," he mutters. "I was held up in class."

"Oh, that's all right. Gave me a chance to kind of stroll down memory lane."

They tentatively reach out to touch hands by way of greeting but stop before any skin contact. He'd almost kissed her during their last visit, his lips at hers, separated by nothing in the air but then he'd slowly drawn away and so had she. They

move toward a partially empty bench, sharing it with an NYU coed chomping down her lunch while cramming for an exam.

"I used to hang out here all the time with Sheldon," she says. "I see some of the same dope dealers and that guy over there—still doing those folk songs."

Now they fall into an uncomfortable silence.

"So what happened?" Jonathan asks.

"It's hard for me to tell you. I don't know myself. You're really the last person I should want to know about this but you're really the only person who can make it clear to me. None of this makes any sense. But you always seem to know what's going on. You're like two different beings—one who sees everything in a wise, objective way and at the same time you're very involved."

"Did something happen with Thaddeus?"

"Yes. He was pushing me on to you."

"Yeah, I sensed that. But why?"

She doesn't want to tell Jonathan about Thaddeus's nasty scheme because Jonathan is still Thaddeus's therapist and Thaddeus needs him more than ever.

"I don't know."

"There has to be a reason."

She can't hold anything back from Jonathan. "He . . . wants something to happen so he can . . . sue the center for malpractice."

"I see," Jonathan answers, outwardly serene, blood boiling inside.

"We fight about that," Beverly tells Jonathan. "No way am I going to set you up like that. Then he makes this phone call and I listen and it's this girl at the office that he's either having an affair with or going to have an affair with. I'm furious. I confront him. He confronts me about you. He knows how I feel. We face each other in like . . . animal rage and then something weird happens. I felt almost out-of-body— like some sort of a transformation swept into me and . . ."

"And . . . ?"

"I'm sorry but I just got crazy with him and he got crazy with me . . . and then we . . . oh God . . . were shocked out of our skulls as it was happening but it was happening as if two other people had taken charge of us except it wasn't other people it was us, maybe the us we saw in each other to begin with . . . I remembered how smart and handsome I thought he was when I first met him. It wasn't no damn American Express that made me marry him. There was something really fine and wonderful there and I guess he saw something in me too.

"Then when it was all over I thought, what have you done to yourself, girl? Are you going to let this so-called black magic moment take over your life? It was like he spooked me, hypnotized me."

The coed finishes her sandwich and folds her book. She glances at the interracial couple sharing the bench with her, frowns, and then leaves. Jonathan, about to hurl his life-changing proposal out there to not only Beverly but to the world, sees the frown as the scorn of society. Actually it's a peptic ulcer, aggravated by the greasy hero sandwich the girl shouldn't have been eating.

He stifles his life-altering speech.

"Listen," Jonathan tells Beverly as he stands to go. "We have a lot of material here to work with." He bends down and kisses her cheek, "At the office."

"That fucking Thaddeus! There I am, to the best of my meager, inexperienced ability trying to help the son of a bitch and all this time he is setting me up to ruin my fucking career."

Jonathan is in his session with Timothy right after his meeting with Beverly.

"More about how you feel about Thaddeus. Unload."

"A low-down fucking snake in the grass. A back stabber. That bastard!"

"Are you holding anything back?"

"A cocksucker. A motherfucka."

"Anything else?"

"No!"

"Really?"

"I said no, dammit!"

"Great!"

"What is so great about it?"

"Not one racial slur."

"Huh?"

"You're seeing him as a real human being. You've worked it through. You can be furious with him, the man, not with that goddamn you know what."

"I'll be a son of a bitch." Jonathan suddenly smiles. "It's true. I don't think of him that way. I'm not a racist anymore!"

Timothy is beaming a rare smile. "I may cancel my sessions with this old Freudian guy now. I was feeling real bad about that session where I called you all those names. I hated doing it though I figured that was what you needed but with this result I am reaffirmed. My instincts were truly sound even though I sounded pretty horrible.

Chapter Ten

Thaddeus and Beverly solemnly move into the office and sit in their customary seats.

Jonathan has been soothing his anxiety over this meeting by telling himself he has not done anything wrong. Nevertheless he fears Thaddeus will denounce him loudly, attracting Luella Peters and possibly Dr. Leonard Warren himself, who has an office only a few doors away. He fears the wrath of the cuckold—although nothing happened . . . a kiss on the cheek . . . what's the big deal. Jonathan imagines Thaddeus is going to reach into his jacket pocket, pull out a subpoena, serve it on him, and then march down the hall to harangue his boss.

"We are in distress because of what has been done to our marriage by your therapist—Mr. Not Yet Doctor (and maybe never going to be after this) Jonathan Meltzer."

Court:

A scathing prosecutor with a hacking voice who looks like Gene Hackman.

"Did you lust after your client *Mrs.* Beverly Carmichael?"

"No." A complete lie—but court is not the place to discuss countertransference adjustments. But he's not a good liar.

His voice rises, eyes shift, if he was taking a lie detector test the blood pressure indicator would shoot up like the hard-on he had when he first saw Beverly.

"Did you ever desire to fondle the breasts of *Mrs.* Beverly Carmichael?" Prosecutor Gene Hackman snarls.

Are you kidding? Did you ever look at those things? What man in his right mind wouldn't want to bury himself there and frolic endlessly?

"No," Jonathan lies through the salivation appearing at the corners of his mouth.

A snicker from every man in court.

Beverly is dressed soberly in a dark suit. Funereal? His? No one has looked anyone in the eye yet. Jonathan clears his throat but can't think of a thing to utter. He'll stay silent in therapeutic sanctuary for the entire session if he has to.

Thaddeus clears his throat, Beverly shifts in her seat. Jonathan suddenly needs to pee.

"This is going to be our last session," Thaddeus announces.

Last session? If that's true, Jonathan's off the hook. Thank God!! But wait they still can sue . . . listen before you leap to a conclusion. He gazes at Beverly who doesn't meet his eye. "We would like to thank you very much for all you've done for us," Thaddeus continues.

"Yes, thank you very much," Beverly intones woodenly.

They seem as if they're not going to sue—relieved, the therapist in Jonathan takes over. "Are all your problems solved?" he probes.

"No, not all of them," Thaddeus replies. "No one's problems are ever completely solved but you've helped us make the kind of beginning we can build on. You helped us discover the things in each other that attracted us to begin with—things we lost in the shuffle with all the anger and resentment. We can talk now, really communicate, and with that we can build a fine marriage with a solid upbringing for our daughter. I'm sure of it and so is Beverly."

Jonathan wants to look at Beverly for confirmation of that last statement but he doesn't dare look her way.

"Another thing," Thaddeus continues. "This is sort of a confession. I've been trying to set you up. It doesn't take a genius to know how you feel about Beverly and I encouraged it. Even lied about her to you. I had a lawyer poised and ready to strike if things went too far. I told myself I did it to make a bundle of money on a settlement but that wasn't the real reason. It's a race thing. Me, a black man, had something that a white man, a Jewish white man, prized. Gave me an inflated feeling of self-importance. I was using your pitiable dilemma to provide me with what I thought was the solution to my life problem—money. But when I found out, not only how I really felt about my wife, but how I really felt about my life, I saw how misguided I was. So with all this I sincerely apologize to you."

"And that's it?" Jonathan asks sharply.

No answer.

"Off into the sunset are you? Happily ever after?"

They're looking at their shoes like children being bawled out.

"You're merely at the beginning of solutions, not the end," Jonathan says. "Okay, I don't think we can work together anymore but let me get you someone else to work with. You can't leave therapy now—you've got to codify what you've learned . . . you've got to . . ."

"I love my husband now," Beverly cuts in. "I've always loved him I suppose but never realized it before. We'll be okay. He's going to leave the insurance business. He can become a wonderful landscape architect. He took some courses years ago and his sketches are beautiful but he was too impatient to stick it out. Now he wants to go back to school, get a degree. He's going to work with a landscape architect, a woman he met when he sold cars. It may be rough for a while, financially, but I'm going back to work to help—my mother will watch Janelle. We'll be fine."

Hypnotized? Drugged? Brainwashed? Jonathan's not sure.

The Carmichaels stand.

"Where are you going?" Jonathan asks. "We still have more time."

"We put the car on a meter?" Thaddeus says. Is there a knowing twinkle in his eye? "We'd like to stop off and tell Dr. Warren about what a great job you did."

"Yes," Beverly says. "Wonderful." Her smile is almost professional, as if she's behind the counter of a spiffy hotel doing a great public relations job on an irate guest. "You're really a fine therapist."

Jonathan watches them file out. What would Timothy do? Bar the door? Call the security guard to not let them out? But he has no strength to stop them. The door closes. They're gone. He'll never see them again. They've formed the core of his existence and now he's without ballast. They're not staying to help him sort out the pieces. And Beverly. She betrayed him.

Later Dr. Leonard Warren calls him into his office and sits him down.

"I want to congratulate you on the Carmichael case," Dr. Warren says. "They were in here before and they couldn't say enough good things about how much you helped them."

Jonathan hasn't had a chance to recover yet. While in a predepression daze he just floated through a session with a methadone client. He was headed for the men's room to throw up before being stopped by Dr. Warren. Now he's seated in front of his boss. He's let the love of his life slip away because of cowardice. And he's ruined her too—she went through that entire charade because he'd hurt her. And now what'll happen to her? Does she really believe all the crap Thaddeus is handing her?

"The beauty part of it is that you did it in ten sessions," Dr. Warren intones with deep satisfaction. "Proves my point. There is virtually nothing that can't be handled in ten well-planned, thought-out, and executed sessions."

Ten? Was it only ten?

Dr. Warren stands and gazes out of his window. He'd renovated the offices so his suite would not face the elevated subway tracks so he now faces the back wall of an office building.

"For a while there I was a little worried," he says with a half laugh. Man-to-man, he glances at Jonathan. "She's really something isn't she?"

Jonathan nods woodenly.

"Can I confess something?" Dr. Warren asks.

Oh, God, another confession!

"I used to get here a bit earlier just so I could watch her come into your office and I always timed a little five-minute break so I could watch her when she came out."

Dr. Warren sits down. "I'll miss her."

Jonathan isn't nauseous anymore. He feels like breaking into an avalanche of tears.

Dr. Warren opens the Carmichael file and glances at it briefly, then takes a deep breath. "There's a new threat to the black community. It's not enough we've got alcohol, drugs, tobacco, STDs, educational deprivation, low expectations, the breakdown of the male super ego, general poverty and malaise, substandard housing, high crime rates, police brutality— no that's not enough. The moment we think there might be a light at the end of the tunnel—a movement underway, affirmative action to correct all the wrongs society has visited on us since we were torn from our homeland—the subtle, devilish *man* has a new one for us, in its way more enslaving and insidious than anything else he has imposed since he brought us here."

Dr. Warren has run out of breath. He pauses for effect. It is effective. Jonathan forgets his sorrow and leans forward. Dr. Warren waits for a question. Jonathan asks, "What is it?"

"Credit card addiction."

"Oh . . ."

"They entice us through advertising with goodies we can't afford and then they make these little plastic magic carpets available to us with these sneaky, hidden, high interest costs."

Dr. Warren pulls an American Express credit card from his wallet and holds it up. "I am an educated, high-income black man! They've lured me into paying a fee for the privilege of going to the brink of bankruptcy. Why? Because I was brought up in poverty and the idea that I can have anything I want immediately is intoxicating. I have bought a fancy car, clothing, furniture I never would have bought without this damn thing. I'm in arrears now. If I don't do something they may take action against me—garnish my income. I am depressed about it, obsessed over it, yet I still charge on it and so does my wife. It's like giving whisky to the Indians. Now if this can happen to me—think of what happens to the poor working stiff black man or the Queens housewife . . . the Beverly Carmichaels. They might as well be back on the plantation humming old African chants.

"Jonathan, you cured Beverly Carmichael of her credit card addiction."

"There's no evidence she's cured," Jonathan mumbles, but Dr. Warren doesn't pay attention.

"I want you to head a program," Dr. Warren states. "We're going to be the first in the state, maybe the first in the nation, to address credit card addiction. I want you to come up with some kind of twelve-step program like AA and Gambler's Anonymous. Credit Card Abusers Anonymous. CCAA. They stand up at a meeting. 'I am a Visa addict. I am an American Express addict! I am a Master Card addict.' There's a big scissors on the platform and the addicts move to the stage with their cards out. Their sponsor holds the card while the addict snips it in half and everyone stands up and cheers. Then stories about ruined lives and careers, broken marriages, delinquent children, on and on. The program becomes famous, emulated by the entire nation—all started here at our little ol' Jamaica Family Center, inaugurated by the center's head, Dr. Leonard Warren, and run by the soon-to-be Dr. Jonathan Meltzer!"

"Why are credit cards so bad?" Jonathan asks.

"A credit card lets you enjoy what you haven't earned yet. It's psychologically debilitating, immature immediate gratification."

"You can go out and make the money to pay the charges," Jonathan replies. "Appetites sometimes create ambition. Some can't handle it but others, many others, will work harder, take courses, whatever it takes. No, thank you. I'm not really interested in running a credit card abuse program."

Maybe he'll call Beverly. He stands but realizes he's not going to. He just needs to go to the bathroom and throw up.

Before leaving he says, "Matter of fact, first thing I'm going to do when I get my doctorate is apply for my own American Express credit card."

Chapter Eleven

Jonathan peers at Arlene through a haze of smoke at the Wilting Flower Bar in SoHo and says, "I guess we ought to get married, huh."

"Is that a question, statement, proposal, or simply a thought provoker?" Arlene replies after licking the salt on the rim of her margarita glass.

"Well, I don't know what it is," he replies.

"Are you drunk?"

"I don't think so . . . and what if I am drunk, so what? Sometimes inebriation allows one to go beyond stifling inhibitions into the higher sphere of real desire. I seriously do want to get married now that my thirties loom so large on my horizon." Jonathan always worries about different stages of life years before he approaches them. He researched acne medication when he was ten years old, a full four years before his first pimple.

"We're still together," he says. "For better or worse, through maze-like convolutions, each of us spilling our psychic, sexual, and spiritual guts to one another with total, sometimes brutal, frankness, yet here we are still seemingly wanting to be in each other's company, in spite of all the jealousy, affairs—on your part, my fantasy doesn't count. No malice—just an observation." He places a sincere hand on her forearm as it rests on the bar rail. "You are a real treasure—a Jewish girl who comes . . . my family will love you with open arms. They hate all this intermarriage. Jew with Christian. Male with male. Female with female. Transsexuals—former boys marrying former girls. No boundaries. *Alle menschen werden brüder!* No clear guidelines anymore on who is no damn good so you mingle with everyone and it's going to be fine a century or so from now but we who are in the vanguard of this revolutionary egalitarianism need some wreckage to cling to as the ship goes down. In spite of my erudition, my advanced degree, my social conscience, I believe in the Jewish male and the Jewish female, mating and finding mutual tsuris as they plunder through life raising little neurotics. It's the life I really want. With you. You're perfect because though Jewish you're basically weird and unpredictable. You'll help me counter the bourgeois little squirt in me I hate so much. In a crumbling world of defecting Jews I'll be a beacon. A Jewish guy at last marrying a Jewish girl with a Jewish, unreconstructed nose and an obviously changed last name."

Arlene Spire. No one who looks like Arlene would come from a family named Spire. It was originally Shapiro.

"Here I am talking seriously, even after three or is it four drinks at a bar—very nontraditional Jewish by the way, buying drinks at a bar at inflated prices like the Irish, spouting out a drunken marriage proposal. God, is it a proposal? I'm scaring myself sober. Maybe it is. All right it is. But I haven't even told you I love you, right? Don't answer. Your aggressive sexual curiosity knowing no bounds. A walking contradiction in terms, a Jewish nymphomaniac yet anchored nevertheless in the deepest Jewish tradition. An Orthodox Jew from an Orthodox family. You'll never fuck on the Sabbath, not even a blow job. I respect that. And you want your children brought up religious but you'll bend a little for me and allow us, if we ever get this together and have children, to bring them up Conservative but not Reform. I respect that. You act like a whore but think like a Hadassah matron from Roslyn Heights.

"As you can probably tell I've been giving this the deepest thought possible. I've applied every possible criterion to this marriage conundrum—psychological of course, logical, spiritual, metaphysical, and philosophical. Me and Timothy are raking this over the coals. Now that he's out of the hospital and amazingly coherent and insightful in ways he never was before—I think it's sometimes right to go crazy because if you come back you're amazing. Sometimes I wish I could let go enough to do that . . . but me I'd have to check my insurance first, rearrange all my appointments, balance my checkbook, and then go nuts. Anyway, Arlene, if we marry I want you to be faithful. I am searching for authenticity. I will be faithful to you. I promise you right here and now.

"We will have children. We will move to Long Island if we have to. Love? Do I love you? I don't know . . . maybe I do or I wouldn't be talking this way. Do you love me? You don't know yourself. It's a question we may never answer. So if we get married and it stinks we'll get a divorce. What's the big deal?"

Arlene is trying to work out of psychedelics into alcohol because she's been frightened of bad trips. But alcohol puts on weight and if she gains maybe another four or five pounds the adjective describing her will turn from zaftig to dumpy. Zaftig gets you hot guys while dumpy only gets you losers who'll screw you only after the really pretty ones are no longer around. Maybe she ought to stop getting high altogether, except whenever she's straight she can't enjoy sex and her entire feeling of self-worth is inextricably tied into her remarkable sexuality without which she's just another Jewish girl looking to get married.

The real reason Arlene's getting desperate to get married is so she can get a breast reduction because these fucking things are weighing her down so much she fears they're going to make her look like a female version of the hunchback of Notre Dame. She can't do it until she gets a guy because guys marry tit. The minute she's got the schmuck, whether it's schmuck Jonathan or any other, she makes an appointment with Dr. Rothstein.

From the very first time she saw them at the age of twelve, Arlene knew they were going to give her trouble. Oh, sure like any prepubescent girl she welcomed them with open chest. Boys would now pay attention to her. Great! Hail tits. I'm so glad you're here. But then she immediately saw her fate as they ballooned. Her mother and sister took after her grandfather's side, modest, not great but sort of okay boobs, but she took after her grandmother's side and that was bad. Her grandmother, now eighty-three, was this little ball of tit with a face on top. Through modern science Arlene won't let that happen to her but now she's getting a little desperate.

"You want another drink? We have the bartender's eye. Here it's on me," Jonathan says magnanimously.

"You paid the last round," Arlene says. They share expenses when they go out. Arlene insists on it. Jonathan playacts like he's simply indulging her but he's delighted to be the recipient of this kind of feminism.

"Let me ask you a question. We just had sex, right?" Arlene says.

Jonathan thinks a moment. "Yeah . . . it was great."

"So why did you pause like you had to remember?"

"I didn't pause because I had to remember, I paused because I'm drinking. When you drink you slow down—anyone knows that."

"I had a disturbing vision when we had sex."

"Go on," Jonathan says, leaning forward.

"I'm not your patient, Jonathan," Arlene rebukes. "Don't treat me like that. I hate it."

"I'm sorry."

"Tonight I opened my eyes and looked at you," Arlene says. "You know studies show most women don't open their eyes while having sex because they're afraid to look at who's actually screwing them. If they do they might realize they're getting *shtupped* by morons. So we tend to focus on a feature we like, hopefully the eyes, but in some cases cheeks or shoulders or in your case your nose—you have a great Roman nose. Your eyes forget about. You look like some bad actor in a movie called *Zombies From Outer Space* because your pupils retreat to the top of your eyeballs and all there is is this big white spooky space. It's like being fucked by the *Night of the Living Dead.* Your nostrils actually turn me on—they're perfectly oval and they are cavernous and flare attractively when you're in your stride."

Arlene is so filthy-mouthed it's embarrassing for Jonathan. She doesn't even lower her voice while mouthing all these obscenities. He's sure she's driven that nice middle-American-looking couple sitting next to them—a cute slender blonde he'd enjoyed looking at—to move away and sit at a little booth that just opened up. He's kicking himself for not grabbing it first because now another couple sits next to them and there's a chance of Arlene offending someone new. He's told her about that kind of thing but when she's a little high she can't stop herself. I don't even know why the fuck I'm talking about marrying her to begin with. What the hell is the matter with me, he thinks.

"You were thinking about her while you were doing it to me!" Arlene snarls. She didn't mean to snarl, she'd have preferred insouciance but it comes out snarl.

"Admit it!"

The couple that just sat down next to Arlene stare and then turn away.

"I can get off in spite of your shallow, transparent performance but tonight it was different. Painfully different. You were screwing her. I could see her curvaceous brown body in the white balloon coming out of your head. She was straddling you and her large, pink-nippled breasts were swaying like pendulums and her beautiful green-hazel eyes . . . —I have the color right, haven't I?—were closed in rapture and her large, lusciously shaped lips were moaning. How she could be so enraptured by that little pickle of yours is beyond me but after all, this was your imagination. Nevertheless you were really there this time, if you know what I mean, even though you weren't there for me but you know what . . . even through my immediate resentment I was happy for a moment that you, you dried up little schlemiel, were capable of such real passion."

Jonathan's appalled because Arlene's on a soap box and the couple who'd been next to her left in the middle of her tirade while the ones who replaced them there are looking at him and shaking their heads slightly while the bartender is visibly contemplating telling them to quiet down especially now that he saw two customers move away. He's afraid that if he tries to quiet her at this stage she'll only get huffy and do something mean and loud.

"And then of course you said her name."
"I did not."

"Oh, Be . . ." Jonathan had moaned.
"What?" Arlene had said.
"What what?"
"What were you saying just now?"
"I was saying oh, beby."
"Beby? What the fuck is beby?"
"It's like oh, baby."
"Oh, baby? You never say oh, baby. It's not in your lexicon. I never get endearments from you Jonathan. There's no, oh, baby, oh, darling, never I love you. There's only a grunt, some spillage and then the inevitable question, 'Did you come?' So what is this 'Oh, beby?'"
"I'm changing. I'm becoming warmer, more giving, more caring."
"Lying bastard, you were going to say oh, Beverly! Come on admit it."
"No way."

He's astounded because Arlene is perfectly accurate, even to the position of the imagined coitus, Beverly straddling him, breasts pendulous, green-hazel eyes. Why the fuck did he have to tell Arlene about the color of Beverly's eyes?! If they ever get married, this crazy Jewish bitch will always bring this detail up to him.

Jonathan was forced to employ fantasy while screwing Arlene this evening because Arlene, attempting to work herself out of drugs, had screwed him completely straight—thereby reverting to her heritage and becoming dry and frigid.

"Listen," Jonathan says. "I think we should call the whole thing off. We have nothing to fight about yet because we're not married but we're fighting like hell."

They've broken up before. Then he goes to singles bars, singles concerts, singles weekends. He does okay. He's a good catch, a young Jewish psychologist. A soon-to-be doctor. Not medical though . . . but still a girl has to consider that letters coming to the house address him as doctor. Dr. and Mrs. Meltzer, not bad. Okay no surgeon so his earnings are not stratospheric but maybe he'll write a great self-help book and make a fortune . . . who knows. He flows into relationships usually with Jewish girls. There's a resurgence of Jews wanting to mate with Jews after almost a generation of out-of-faith Jewish marriages, if you want to call modern American Judaism a faith.

(Jonathan doesn't think of Judaism as a faith, it's more like an automobile club, AAA. You hope you never need them but if you do they're there for marriage, death, and kaddish.)

Aside from the Orthodox, no modern American Jew has faith in anything Jewish except Israel, which is so pugnaciously Jewish it's almost bar-brawl Irish. When Jonathan went to Israel for a week with his parents when he was nineteen he wanted to get the hell out lest someone stick a rifle in his hands. The Orthodox frighten him because they believe all other Jews, especially Jews like him, are basically no damn good. He's afraid they'll come with white robes one dark night burning a Star of David on his lawn in Merrick, Long Island, and string him up on the big pine tree that's too much like a Christmas tree on the front lawn.

So he's dated a Deidre and gone to bed with a Jessica and performed some weird oral things with an Ariel but somehow he always hooks back with Arlene. There's a comforting cognitive dissonance about her. She's incredibly weird but underneath there's no one more bourgeoisie than Arlene.

Arlene broods at the bar. Maybe it's her fault, encouraging and most of the time frankly enjoying all this openness with Jonathan—especially telling him imagined adventures. She can tell him anything about herself. He always comes back. Oh, sure he bristles about this or that but he feels professionally motivated to hear everything. He's feeling the need to get married and she ought to jump on it except for this Beverly thing. She didn't need to hear from him that he'd fallen in love with that damn woman. And he didn't need to infer— that *momser,* little pickle motherfucka—that he would never get over Beverly in his entire life. That was crossing the line. How could he expect to have any future with her with such a shadow between them?

They sit for a while wondering what to do next.

"You slept with *fagella* Craig but I never bring it up to you, do I?" Jonathan says. "Even though that hurt like hell."

"Nothing happened."

"Through no fault of your own."

Jonathan wasn't really hurt. When he thinks about Arlene and Craig he almost breaks out in laughter. He pictures Arlene stooped over Craig's flaccid member, yanking, pulling, stroking, sucking, beseeching with nothing much happening.

"I'd marry you if I knew you were really over Beverly," she says. "I really would. I love you."

Did she actually say that? Does she mean it? Does she want to marry this schmuck, this little dick rapid-fire putz? She doesn't really respect the nebbish, doesn't think he's particularly cute or smart even with his advanced degree. Trouble is there's no real edge to him. She likes guys who make her a little nervous . . . she likes a sense of danger though, God forbid danger itself. The only real edge Jonathan putzface has is this thing with Beverly.

"I am over her. I told you that," Jonathan says.

"Tell me again."

"I don't think about her anymore."

"Bullshit."

"Okay, bullshit . . . whatever . . ."

"You know what? I don't believe you, but we'll go along with it anyway. Like you said, we can always get a divorce. If there are kids, what the hell, most kids in their class will come from divorced parents anyway so they won't feel ostracized."

"So what are we going to do now? You want to get engaged?"

"I have to now meet the wicked witch of Antarctica, and her husband Mr. No Spine, and your two other siblings, is that right?"

"You may not want to marry me after you meet my mother."

"I'll bring my mother along and let them battle it out and we'll make a bet as to whose mother is nastier and more aggressive."

"I give you odds on mine. Listen, can't we just elope or some shit like that. I don't want to go through all this stuff."

"Me neither."

"But I guess we've got to, right?"

"I guess."

"The question is, will you still be a good lay as my fiancée and then as my wife?"

"That is a good question. I may revert to kind and dry up. And you may always have to think about your fucking Beverly. Is this how we're going to have to go through life?"

"Maybe."

"So are we enraged already?"

"It's engaged, not enraged."

"Oh? Yeah."

So Jonathan has received a qualified yes to his proposal of marriage. Has he had five drinks instead of three? Can he claim drunkenness?

They sit awhile contemplating the crowd in the SoHo bar. There're five good-looking girls, counting two waitresses, two dining with guys, and a girl walking by, each of them cuter than Arlene, Jonathan thinks. They're probably traditional and sweet—want a steady, good guy, kids, and financial security. All but one looks like a shiksa so there's no problem with them coming and stuff. If any have emotional problems he can deal with them effectively because, after all, he's in the business.

"Hey, listen," Arlene says, patting his arm. "Don't let it worry you. I'm not ready to commit anyway."

They're close to an agreement but there's a barrier.

"We've like established our parameters, so to speak," Jonathan replies. "We kind of both know where we're at."

"I want an open marriage. I don't want to wear a wedding ring," Arlene says.

"An open marriage is bad for children."

"Hey, listen, we'll worry about it when it happens. Remember, an open marriage means that both of us can . . ."

"I know what it means."

Arlene plans on being much sexier when she finally hooks Jonathan. Not only is she going to get a breast reduction but she's going to straighten her teeth, get a nose job, and maybe a little preemptive face work. There'll be no reason then to waste all that feminine power on one little schlemiel. She would do it now except she has no money and Jonathan's father is getting rich off the stock market. No Jewish father will deny his son money to fix his daughter-in law's teeth though you'd have to hide breast reduction in the budget because no Jewish father-in-law would want to pay for that.

"Can I ask you how come you popped the hypothesis tonight? Really?" Arlene asks.

Jonathan, realizing what he has just done—PROPOSED MARRIAGE—says, "I got to throw up."

Chapter Twelve

Dr. Jonathan Meltzer is strolling up Jamaica Avenue. When he was uncomfortable in an all-black neighborhood he'd simply leave his office building, turn left, eat at the diner on the corner, and return to his office. Then after work he'd get on the train or into his father's car and drive away. But now he enjoys the buzz of the dense, teeming shopping area. He eats at different places—a Chinese restaurant, a pizza joint, a coffee shop. He makes a mental note to mention his new-found ease to Timothy on his next visit to Payne Whitney, the psychiatric section of New York Hospital, where Timothy is again an inpatient because his plastic-loving, unpantheistic, Indian girlfriend, Suzy, redumped him and he apparently attempted suicide with a massive dose of every drug he could lay his hands on—at least according to the rumor going around school.

When Jonathan first heard, he rushed to visit. He found Timothy in the rec room hammering out a fairly decent, though rust-fingered, version of "The Entertainer." Timothy finished the piece, turned, fixed him with a heavy-lidded gaze, and asked, "Well, how did it go this week?"

So Timothy wasn't going to acknowledge the new relationship—not going to be an inpatient in a nut house at least as far as his outpatient Jonathan was concerned.

"Pretty well." Jonathan picking right up on it. "I think I'm finally getting over her." He gazed at Timothy to see if Timothy really knew whom he meant.

"Really?" Timothy said.

"I hardly think about Janelle anymore . . ." Jonathan testing Timothy.

"Janelle? I thought her name's Beverly."

"Oh, yes, Janelle's her daughter's name. I mean, of course, Beverly."

They moved away from the piano and sat on a couch.

"I started to see Arlene again. I told her all about Beverly. She's very understanding, really nice. She had a thing too. This guy she's sharing her pad with—he's gay and she tried to convert him."

Jonathan's working at NYU Medical Center, assisting in group-geriatric counseling as well as individual therapy. His parents will loan him money to set up an office downtown to start his own practice. He knows a number of young, starting-out doctors who'll refer cases to him. He intends to keep his association with the Jamaica Family Center because he feels the experience is invaluable and he's socially committed, even though he realistically doesn't expect any private referrals because most of the clientele do not have the wherewithal.

As he passes a shop, Maternally Yours, he catches a glimpse of the browsing form of what might be a familiar female at a clothing rack. He feels a heart squeeze. It could be Beverly. He pauses.

He shouldn't want to see Beverly. His life is going well right now. He feels really good. He's personally gone through a "lost-love" experience so his professional empathy and perception of similar experiences can be even deeper. The scab is formed and there's no reason to rip at it.

He moves on. Then pauses again.

What is she doing, if it is Beverly, looking for maternity clothes? She certainly could not be having another child with Thaddeus, could she? That would be disastrous. She would have to get rid of Thaddeus to be happy, not have another kid with him. Jonathan never bought that newborn love nonsense. There could be nothing but misery ahead for her. The last thing he thought might happen would be her becoming pregnant. But what if he's wrong? Could it be happy-ever-after?

If so, he doubts he's in the right end of his profession. He still could go into research if he has such little understanding of people. He must find out. He's going back to see if it is Beverly.

But no, wait, if he has been wrong it's because he'd fallen in love, so how could he be objective?

It would truly be disastrous, from any perspective, to now run into Beverly. He knows that for sure.

Beverly isn't showing yet. She's checking out the style and prices of maternity clothes but isn't sure she'll bother because they're awfully expensive and smart women are into wearing smocks and loose slacks now. She's not charging stuff anymore because things are too tight now.

She's seen Jonathan and turns away hoping he'll pass. She's ashamed of being pregnant. Why did he have to catch her shopping at Maternally Yours?!

But then she can't let him pass. She moves toward the window of the store. He can't pass her by either. They smile at each other. Jonathan watches her approach, marveling at how beautiful she is. They face each other, take each other's hand, then, in spite of where they are, a crowded, sunny shopping street, teeming with people in an area not accustomed to interracial couples, they kiss. They gaze into each other's eyes—her green-hazel and his deep blue.

"How are you?" he asks. He's dizzy from her proximity and the magical touch of her lips. He leans against the window, oblivious to a woman who wants to see the latest low-cut maternity model on display.

"I'm fine . . . now . . ." she says softly. They pause awhile not able to say anything at all. Finally Jonathan asks, "How are things working out?"

"He left me," she says, attempting to keep the hurt out. "He's living with a girl from his old insurance office. You were right. We should have continued therapy with someone else. He's so confused now—sometimes thinks he's still in love with me but really obsessed with this girl. Going crazy with all the changes he's trying to make in himself—like all at one time . . . nothing gradual . . . constantly at war with what he calls his old self and new self. Me, I'm part of the old and she's part of the new . . . crazy stuff like that. Meanwhile he's not earning enough to send anything for his daughter so I need to go to work except . . ."

He looks significantly at the store they've just come from.

"Yeah," she says. "I'm pregnant."

They start to walk casually. She takes his hand in hers.

"With all that, I can't stop thinking about you," she says. "When I saw you just now I realized I've been shopping down here because I wanted to run into you. That's why I should have continued therapy with someone else—to get over you . . . I was really very foolish. Jonathan, say something please."

He can't say a word.

"Jonathan, take me to a hotel," she says. "I want to have one time with you—just one so I can remember it the rest of my life. I know we can't be together—I know there are too many obstacles . . . but that doesn't mean we can't . . . each of us have one beautiful memory in our lives."

One time with her. Just one to remember the rest of his life. No complications. An afternoon of lovemaking he can take to the grave. But can he make love to her once and then go on his way? The touch of her hand, the feel of her lips, listening to her voice. She is his erotic and spiritual soul mate.

But he'll want much more. A woman soon with two kids—not his. What if he falls so much in love he winds up marrying her? Now he's a stepfather and the real father is that son of a bitch Thaddeus. What genes will he have to deal with? He doesn't even want his own kids until he's maybe forty much less someone else's and . . . he can't help this thought . . . of a different race. A race with problems.

All right, so schmuck, what's the big deal? Take her to a hotel, make love to her like crazy, and then good-bye. Just like she says—it's too complicated and not practical. She just wants you to make love to her once. Coast clear. She's not a client and she's not with her husband. And you're not—as they say, "committed."

But just once would plant the commitment in his bones, his libido, his heart. He would lie in bed with her, stroking her beautiful body, and he would know he loved her and he would tell her he loved her and she would tell him she loved him and he would be fucking fucked!

She's waiting for an answer. He looks into her exquisite, pliant, green-hazel eyes and says, "Yes!"

He takes her hand and starts walking toward the parking lot where he has his car. They stop at a busy street crossing.

There's a black cop directing traffic. The cop is staring at him holding Beverly's hand.

A bolt of fear strikes Jonathan. He lowers his eyes. He almost releases her hand but then he thinks—hey we're not in the Deep South during the Jim Crow years so he continues to hold her hand but only a little more lightly. When the light changes he makes sure not to look at the cop as they cross the street.

Beverly's used to being stared at harshly from her time with Sheldon. She looks that cop right in the eye and sort of smirks at him as they cross the street. She thinks of what Thaddeus might say—eat shit, motherfucka!

I'm going to get him but will I want him? Beverly thinks. Sure I can make him really fall in love with me but will he want to marry me? And even if he does, will his family butt in? Of course they will—just like Sheldon's family—and she didn't have any kids then. I'm letting myself in for another crushing disappointment.

She wants to stop and tell him to forget it, maybe shake hands or even a little peck on the cheek and go on her way but almost as if he reads her thoughts he tightens the pressure of his hand and she moves on without a word.

His fantasy is about to become real! He recalls a session with crazy but wise Timothy.

"Tell me," Timothy asked. "Any regrets about not making love to Beverly?"

"Regrets, no. How about deep sorrow? How about tears in the night, how about haunting dreams, how about being caught unawares when some random thing reminds me of her—some smile like hers or some curve of a cheek . . ."

"You should have fucked her. You were an idiot," Timothy said.

"No, I did the right thing."

"You mean the ethical thing?"

"Correct."

"Thou can never fuck a former client until two years have passed since she's out of treatment, according to the ethics of the American Psychological Association."

"I could not have made love to that woman once and then walked away. I know me. I would be in love irretrievably, in heat, in mania, fixated. One afternoon in a hotel with Beverly! You must be kidding. That would be like Faust signing on the dotted line."

"The best way to get over a fantasy is to fuck it. A perfect body in your imagination has a lump here and cellulite there. Breasts suspended into the stratosphere, once the marvelously engineered bra is snapped, plummet like boulders in an avalanche. Her sweet nothings in your ear become gibberish. Oh, it's fine of course, it's great but it becomes what it really is. A simple sexual encounter. By fucking her you take the magic out of it. You can then peer at it logically. Is this what I want to plunge myself into for life? Stepfather to a kid, an interracial thing you're not at all ready for, a former client whose husband can ruin you professionally? But no, you didn't do that. Your cowardice fucked you up and now you're a victim of 'what could have been' and you'll never be able to prove yourself right or wrong. Jonathan, you are indeed picking up the bar tab here so at the risk of biting the hand that's been getting me drunk I have to say—you were an unqualified schmuck."

Okay, Timothy, now it's happening! And I feel great. Fuck the American Psychological Association!

Jonathan remembers that, according to Thaddeus, Beverly doesn't like motels. She likes hotels—fancy, expensive hotels—but he doesn't know of one hotel in Queens, not one! What a fucking low-life borough! Oh, shit does he have his father's American Express card on him?! Yeah, he does, he remembers. He'll have to drive into the city for a nice hotel and park in a garage and pay New York City prices. His mother, who still takes care of all the bills, will have a fit when she sees the charges even though he always pays for what he runs up.

"So why didn't you take this person to a Queens motel where they have parking and a room for a couple of hours at maybe eighty dollars?

"And so who is this person that you spend $300 on? Is it a serious relationship? Why don't you bring her here? You still have your own room with your own entrance." And then he knows what she'll ask, because she's been getting worried not only about him but society in general—about the prevalence of what to her is a pestilence.

"Is it a man, a gay, is that why you don't want to . . . ?"

"No, mother it was not a man. I am not gay!"

"All right, all right, I'm just asking."

They reach his car, or he should say his father's car. They get in. There's no one in the parking lot. He feels the pull of her presence. He turns to her. She is looking straight ahead. He looks at her tummy and there's no sign of her being pregnant yet. He shifts his body closer to her. She's not looking at him but she feels his closeness—his breath upon her cheek. And then he puts his arm around her shoulder. She turns to him and looks at him compliantly. He pauses. Her lips part slightly. They begin to kiss ardently. Her arms go around his neck and she draws him close to her. She caresses his face. His left hand fondles her breast as his right hand slides down her back. He snakes his hand under her slacks and then under her panties onto her behind. And the moment his hand slips under her panties he feels something rising. He's coming!!!

He pulls his hand off her ass and the other hand off her breast. He holds his breath. He dare not even look at her. He wills himself to calm down, but it's too late. His penis is rat-tat-tatting his stuff unashamedly into his underwear.

What happened? Why did he stop so suddenly? They don't know what to say. They don't look at each other.

Did he? Could he have . . . ? Omigod! It was the same with Sheldon, she recalls. What the hell is the matter with these Jewish guys?! Their mothers are so damn bitchy and bossy that they get overwhelmed when a nice, warm sexy woman comes along. Damn!

It took her an infinite amount of patience before she could get a good fuck out of Sheldon. He came so goddamn fast that it was over even before it began. But at least he came while doing it, but it looks like this damn guy couldn't even wait for that. And now if they go someplace, she's going to have to wait till he can get it up again but she has to be home to relieve her mother from watching Janelle. That means driving to some cheap-ass, smelly Queen's motel instead of maybe the Hyatt in Manhattan and then waiting for this guy to get it up so that she can have him give her at least a respectable fuck. Maybe she should call her mother and tell her she's running late. This could be important. Even though this Jonathan can't hold his fire she could maybe let herself fall in love with him because he's so cute and smart and Jewish. She could teach him how to fuck a little better as time went on. After a while he'd be used to her so that it might make him last maybe two or possibly three minutes—one time Sheldon was at it for maybe five or six minutes—a Jewish guy's Hall of Fame record.

That no good for nothing ex Mr. Thaddeus no good Carmichael, say what you want about him but he sure knew how to pleasure a woman. She would come like a machine gun with that no good son of a bitch. And as nasty as he was in normal life, while fucking, all kinds of darlings and sweeties and endearments dropped from his false tongue like rain. Even though she knew he was a phony she relished every endearment.

Why is life like that? You find a man who can fuck and he's no damn good. You find a man that's really good and he can't fuck!

Why do I need these guys anyway!?

Sometimes I wish I could turn queer like my friend Ellie. Women are so nice, so sweet. Trouble is I can't get no satisfaction, like the Stones say, with a woman. Kissing one and letting them touch me—ugh. And just my bad luck the one man who can really do it for me is a no good son of a bitch while the one man I crave, for now anyway, is a fucking dud.

Shit!

This might be her last chance to marry a nice Jewish guy and live out on the North Shore of Long Island. Sheldon at his best was a damn piss-poor lover too but she loved him anyway.

She pictured herself out on the North Shore maybe at first Roslyn and then as her Jonathan made more money, the ultimate—Great Neck! She'd find herself a deliveryman or postman or any damn man that could do it right to come by when the kids are off to school.

She could have it all!!!

"What's the matter?" Beverly asks.

"I . . . I . . ." Jonathan mutters.

He's in a jam. Should he confess that he came in his pants but then there's that voice in his head, "Hey, you can't tell a woman that! I mean do you want her to diaper you or fuck you?"

Maybe I can tell her I'm enraged, I mean engaged. Jonathan clears his throat as if he's about to make a speech. Beverly waits. He changes his mind. He doesn't want to tell her that.

Maybe I can explain what happened, tell her she's so beautiful and desirable that I couldn't contain myself.

Then a voice comes ringing in his head out of nowhere. It almost sounds like her damn ex-husband Thaddeus Carmichael.

Jewboy's love song. My dick's too small, I come too fast, I fart too much, I belch, I'm constipated, I have colitis, my nose's too big, my lips too thin. Listen man, do you want to really learn how to fuck a woman—I mean really make love to her so that that woman can't get enough of you. Tell her how beautiful she is, you tell her she ought to be a movie star, a top model, on the cover of *Vogue* . . . you tell her when you make it big you going to cover her pretty ass in diamonds and pearls and furs . . . you tell her that you gonna buy her the biggest house in Great Neck, this bitch loves Great Neck. You tell her shit like that and before you know it she'll imagine your dick's the size of Derek Jeter's baseball bat.

"It's unethical," Jonathan blurts out.

"What is?"

"Look, I-I'm crazy about you. I think I fell in love with you the moment I saw you come into my office. I'm sorry. It's crazy I know. But I was your therapist. Any sexual relationship a therapist has with a former patient is unethical until at least two years have passed that they've been out of treatment."

She turns to Jonathan and smiles softly at him. "Jonathan, I respect your honesty and integrity. I had no idea that even after the therapy is over it's illegal for us to have anything to do with each other."

"Well it's not, strictly speaking, illegal, just unethical."

"You mean you wouldn't go to jail?"

"Oh, no, of course not. If something had happened during the therapeutic relationship one could bring a civil suit against the therapist and in this case the Jamaica Family Center but now it's just a matter of ethics," he says weakly.

"Ethics? Is that what you said—ethics?"

"Yes, ethics."

"Well, I wouldn't want you to do anything that would violate your ethics. Would you take me home, please?"

"You're angry?"

"Not at all. But I wonder why didn't you invoke your ethics before?"

"I couldn't stop myself."

"But you're able to stop yourself now?"

Did she glance down at his pants when she said that?

They reach Beverly's house. She has to rush so she gives him a quick but hot kiss and dashes out. Jonathan can't help noticing the landscape around the house, especially compared to the neighboring homes. There's a lovely garden in the front and the bushes are full, trimmed and really neat. That couldn't be Thaddeus's handiwork, could it? And then as he was about to pull away, he saw what must be Beverly's mother hurriedly leave the house.

The woman is the spitting image of Beverly only older but not much older. He can't help a flash image of Arlene's mother from popping into his head. Arlene's mother is ravaged by too much work—too much liposuction, reconstruction, and Botox.

Beverly's mother smiles and greets a passing neighbor.

Arlene herself simply ignores her neighbors unless they're gay males and then she becomes sloppily friendly.

Jonathan fights to calm himself. He's becoming carried away. He looks out at the neighborhood. If he married Beverly they could live wherever they wanted.

Chapter Thirteen

Jonathan's next session with Timothy is after his debacle with Beverly. He's tortured. He needs to talk about what happened and be totally honest. Damn.

It's early afternoon in their favorite SoHo bar. Jonathan light beer. Timothy straight gin—not even on the rocks. Timothy looks clean, shaven, and sober—for now.

Jonathan feels guilty that he's not going to invite Timothy to his wedding. He wants to, but Arlene won't allow it.

"You don't invite your fucking shrink to your wedding, Jonathan, especially a nutcase like Timothy. I can see it now, the rabbi looks out at the congregation and says, 'If there's anyone here who objects to this wedding, let us hear it now or forever hold your peace.' And this nutcase Timothy stands up and yells, 'Stop the wedding, the groom hasn't worked through his prebirth neurosis yet plus his not-so-latent homosexual doppelganger!'"

"Darling," Jonathan replied patiently, "Jews don't do that and you know it."

"No Timothy at our wedding!" Arlene insisted.

"Listen, I want him to meet my beautiful bride so that when I complain about you he can have a picture in his head of what you look like."

"No Timothy at our wedding! That's final!"

Timothy starts light. "So how was the Colorado ski trip?"

"Fine," he states with an up in his voice. "The skiing was great."

"Um-huh."

"Yeah, great."

Jonathan becomes uncomfortable. He knows he should talk about his "stuff." God knows he has plenty of "stuff" to talk about but all at once he feels stupid and incompetent.

Timothy is waiting. Jonathan has to . . . has to . . . here goes . . .

"I ran into Beverly yesterday," he mumbles.

"What?"

"I ran into Beverly yesterday."

"Beverly who?"

"The wife of that former client of mine . . . you know . . ."

"Um-huh, go on."

Now Timothy is acting like a real shrink. He's nodding um-huh and telling Jonathan to go on. In a way that's scarier than when he's a little berserk.

"We chatted a bit . . ."

"Um-huh."

"Anyway she told me that she wanted to be with me . . ."

"Oh?"

"Just one time, she said. She wanted to create a time that we could take with us forever. She knew there were too many practicalities to our really being together but at least we could have that one beautiful time that we could take with us through eternity."

Of course Beverly didn't quite put it that way but Jonathan couldn't help the embellishment.

"That's lovely," Timothy sighs. "Did she really say that?"

"Well, something like that."

"What a wonderful woman. Go on."

"I took her hand and we walked to my car. There I was a white guy in pretty much an all-black neighborhood and I was scared. A black cop looked at me as if he wanted to arrest me but I still held on to her hand."

Actually he'd moved from holding her hand to holding her elbow, which is not quite the same thing, but he's still being basically honest.

"Good for you," Timothy says. A new Timothy, encouraging, supportive. Wow.

"We walked to my car and got in. Actually it's my father's car but anyway we got in."

Timothy is totally enthralled. He's even neglecting his drink.

"Uh-huh, go on."

"We say nothing for a while, we're suddenly timid, tentative."

"Yes, of course."

"And then we simultaneously turn. We slowly move toward each other and then there's that moment that I'd been fantasizing about—our first kiss."

"Ah . . . yes."

"Then we're into it, our tongues intertwining like two snakes. I rest my left hand on her cheek and she puts her arms around my neck."

Jonathan pauses, remembering.

"Go on."

"Then I put my left hand on her right breast."

"Ahhh . . ."

"Timothy, in all my life I have never felt a breast like that. How it could be so firm yet so yielding . . ."

"Suzy's breasts were like that . . ."

Jonathan plunges ahead before Timothy gets started on one of his endless Suzy interruptions.

"Then my right hand slides down her back and my hand goes under her slacks, slips into her panties . . ."

"Go on."

"And then my hand goes all the way down on her behind . . ."

"Yeah and then?"

"I come in my fucking pants!"

"Fuck no!"

"Fuck yes."

Jonathan awaits the inevitable castigation. He can almost write it—what kind of a schmuck are you?! You get a beautiful woman who wants to fuck you, God only knows why, and first thing you do is come in your fucking pants?!

But Timothy says, "Same thing happened to me the first time I touched Suzy's cunt."

Jonathan can hardly believe he's heard that. They sit silently sulking, then Timothy starts talking.

"I finally got over the disgrace of it, the shame of it, the embarrassment. They know what happened even though they don't say anything about it."

Beverly had played it real cool, a real class act. But what if it had been Arlene! He gets a harrowing image of Arlene somehow pulling down his pants, yanking his wet underwear off, then running into the street shouting, "Look at what Dr. Jonathan Meltzer did! Look at what Dr. Jonathan Meltzer did!"

Jonathan orders a Scotch on the rocks.

"Turned out," Timothy says, "that was one of the best things that ever happened to me. I was able to get in touch with my little lost boy, the little baby who couldn't get enough of his mother's breast, the little boy who only sees the world as a place to either nourish him or deny him. He's not supposed to be a hungry little boy anymore. He's a big guy. He needs to give as well as receive. He has to perceive on a very deep emotional level that the woman he's making love to has her needs and desires too and that she is looking for a man, not a little love-starved boy.

"It's not just sexual. You become a good lover when you become a real mensch, when you're not looking for every relationship, man or woman, to nourish that poor little baby boy you should have left behind years ago. Don't look at me that way, Jonathan. Sure, I'm not there yet or I wouldn't drink so much and I wouldn't have lost my sweet little Suzy and my life would be a hell of a lot more together. But I want to help you get there. By helping you get there I'll be putting myself that much closer."

Timothy is in tears. And so is Jonathan. They embrace, right there at the bar—man-to-man.

Chapter Fourteen

Arlene would like to fuck Craig. Since the first time she laid eyes on him she has wanted to fuck him. If you fuck a gay guy it's missionary work, redemption, God's work. A mitzvah.

"I hated gays," Craig has told Arlene. "I absolutely hated them. Of all my gang of tough kids I was the worse. I'd join in leering at the girls with the other kids and I put on such a good act that I later decided to be an actor. But I began to suspect it was only an act and I became very depressed without really knowing why and even considered suicide at one point. I had no one to turn to, had no idea what was really wrong with me."

"What was it that made you aware you were gay?"

"One day my friends Mel and Billy got this girl Elaine to come over when my parents weren't home. We all got high and listened to music and danced and drank beer and before you know it Mel and Elaine were doing it right on my bed with me and Billy looking on. Elaine was smiling at us sort of beckoning us to join them. It was really hot and crazy and, before you know it, me and Billy sort of got into each other's eyes. I still didn't have an erection until I saw Billy's erection and then . . . well . . . that was the most magic moment in my life. It all cleared up for me—in a huge clairvoyant flash. I just jumped between Billy's legs and took him in my mouth. I can't describe that feeling of coming home. I didn't care that Mel and Elaine were gawking at us, their faces filled with shock."

"And?"

"After that I was ostracized but I didn't care, my life as a gay man had begun."

Arlene wants to convert Craig. She would dump Jonathan in a flash. She would marry Craig. She would love to have children with him because he's beautiful in every way. She's looked up gay conversion on the Internet and all she found was some religious bullshit and not even in her own religion. Only Christians believe in that gay conversion shit, Jews are too smart. She's been trying to make Craig discover his inner heterosexual.

They're in Craig's new apartment in the West Village. Craig has just landed a soap and he's borrowed against his future earnings to get a real high-priced West Village one-bedroom pad for himself.

He's in a real dilemma concerning Arlene. He's really, truly in love with her—has been from almost the first time he met her. There's something about those big bazooms of hers and that air of feminine confidence that has always gotten to him—even on an erotic basis although he's been careful to hide that fact from both himself and her.

She has, of course, tried her best to seduce him. She has walked around bare-chested in front of him, put her hands all the way up on his thigh. Confessed not only her love for him but her lust as well.

But now that she is engaged he's beginning to feel that he's losing her and he's becoming uneasy in her presence. There they are sitting on his couch in the midafternoon. She has stopped by after calling him in the middle of the day taking a break from her round of calls as an accountant for the firm of Bernstein, O'Hara and Simmons.

She is showing him pictures of her skiing trip—she and her fiancé, Jonathan, smiling and very happy. Craig suddenly feels a pang or two, which he reluctantly acknowledges as jealousy. He tries to dismiss the feeling but then Arlene starts to go into detail about the suite they were in. The hotel made a mistake and they found themselves in the bridal suite for two nights. She shows him pictures of a canopied bed, a bathroom with a Jacuzzi and a sauna and then she shows him a naughty video selfie of her and Jonathan cavorting around with hardly any clothes on and then some intimate ones with no clothes on.

Then this crazy, vixen accountant shows him a video that has Arlene spread in bed with this Jonathan, a guy that never impressed him as much, crouching on top of her, obviously about to enter her with his version of a hard-on. Craig is appalled, not at the bad taste of Arlene taking this selfie and showing it to him. Oh no, he's appalled at the size of the guy's wiener. Not that he's stunted but he's shamefully ordinary. Is this what a woman like Arlene is going to have to settle for the rest of her life?

He keeps staring at that dirty video. Arlene laughing, and this jerky-looking guy with a serious look on his face about to have sexual intercourse with the woman, he suddenly realizes, he's been in love with all along.

He looks at Arlene. She has both a twinkle and an invitation in her eye. He makes a move to get off the sofa but she grabs his wrist and compels him to look at her. Arlene's lips are moist. He's kissed Arlene before but more or less jokingly but this time there's no joke in the air. He again moves to get off the couch but she holds his wrist firmly. The selfie flashes in his head.

Before he knows it her blouse and bra are off. He wonders how that happened. Did he pull off her blouse and unhook her bra?

Is he hot for her? There he is acting like a real guy—kissing, touching, feeling. Is he just goofing her? How far will he go?!!

Craig doesn't really know what's going on with him. He's really hot.

Somehow before they both realize it they are out of their clothes really going at each other.

Craig is now at full mast, down down down he goes round round round he goes in a spin knowing that spin he's in feeling that old black magic called . . . love. (old song)

When he realizes that the entire experience of fucking a woman he loves will destroy his life as a gay man.

He thinks of Corcoran, the assistant director of his soap— without their affair he never would have gotten that part. All the gay camaraderie gone. All the casual affairs gone. All the fun gone. The mortgage, the kids, and worst of all the sup- posed fidelity to one person for the rest of your then very dreary fucking life!

Craig gets out of his crouch and stands up. He moves into the bathroom and locks the door.

Arlene, stunned, lies there awhile until she realizes he's not coming back. She gets dressed and leaves the apartment.

Chapter Fifteen

The next evening finds Arlene and Jonathan at the same bar drinking margaritas.

Arlene is preoccupied with a spreadsheet.

"What are you doing?" Jonathan asks.

"I want to show you something."

"You don't put a spreadsheet on a bar. The only thing you should put on a bar is drinks, elbows, and money."

"I just want to show you something."

"I never can get the hang of spreadsheets, Arlene."

"It's simple." She lays out the spreadsheet.

"This is my income and this is your income, right here. This is our expenses, to the penny, of course allowing leeway and flexibility."

"Can't be to the penny if you allow leeway and flexibility."

"You know what I mean. Now here's our savings as of today."

"What do you mean as of today?"

"We're invested in mutual funds, Jonathan, you know these four guys each holding each other's wrists."

"Is that four guys or two do you think?"

"Two couldn't do it."

"I always kind of felt it was like a bunch of guys preventing each other from hitting each other—like arms control," Jonathan says smugly.

"That's an interesting association. Why don't you save it for your next session with nutcase Timothy? Instead of them joining in mutual cooperation you have them in a type of arms control. The aggressive underpinning of your association is fascinating."

"You're beginning to sound like me."

"Jonathan, here look . . ."

"Not now."

"Why not now?"

"I'm drinking, Arlene, damn it."

"You're tense. Something wrong?"

"No."

"You know, Jonathan, it is today that I consider our half-year anniversary. It'll happen in a few more seconds."

Arlene is looking at her wristwatch.

"What will?"

"The exact moment we became enraged."

"You timed it?"

"Yes, I did. After we said it was settled you had to throw up and when you left I took a look at my watch and it was 10:04 P.M. Wait . . ."

She counts down. "There it is. Happy half-year enragement anniversary, darling."

They kiss. Arlene fully committed, Jonathan kind of faking it.

"Well a half year later." Arlene cuddling up. "What do you think?"

"Great."

"Uh-huh."

"Yeah, great."

"Great, right?"

"Yeah, great."

"So why am I so pissed off now?"

"Pissed off?"

"Your 'great' sounded so phony," Arlene snaps. "You don't think it's been great?"

"Yeah, no, it's great."

"Everything's great?"

"Yeah, just great."

"Nothing wrong?"

"Absolutely not. Perfect."

Jonathan gulps down the remainder of his drink. "I need to tell you something," he blurts from the bottom of his tortured soul.

"What?"

"Let me get another drink first." Jonathan orders another round.

"Okay, so?"

"Wait till the drink comes."

"You need a drink before you tell me something? You need to bolster your courage?"

"Of course not."

"I hate that you're always so afraid of me. Try telling me what you want to tell me without a drink."

"You're so damn bossy."

"You're so damned scared of me."

"I'm not scared of you."

"I'm not scared of you," Arlene mocks. "Listen to that pitiful, defensive whine. You're always afraid I'm going to make you do something you don't want to do. It's like I'm the worst bitch in the world. I hate that."

"I don't need a drink to tell you something. I want a drink."

"You need a drink."

"No, I want a drink."

"A need challenged becomes a want."

"No, I just want a drink first."

"First?"

"I just want a drink!"

The drinks come.

"Okay, have your drink and then tell me. Feel the liquid surge down your cowardly gullet giving you courage as it flows down into your gutless gut."

"Hey, that was pretty good . . . 'cowardly gullet giving you courage as it flows down into your gutless gut.'"

"Remember I was an English major before I was an accountant."

"How could you go from being an English major to becoming an accountant?"

"There's more poetry and drama in numbers than most of the novels they publish today."

"Right."

"Okay, then drink up and tell me."

"I don't have to drink up in order to tell you. It'll stay right in front of me untouched and I will tell you what I need to tell you."

"Typical passive putz behavior. First fear, then adamant denial. Jonathan, I don't want you to turn into a total passive putz. I hate passive men. I hate pussy-whipped men, spineless turds who are so afraid of being castigated, humiliated, and dominated by a woman—whether it's mother, wife, sister, girlfriend, teacher, waitress, barmaid—in short, anything in a skirt. If you allow yourself to become a real passive putz you lose your identity, strength of character, resolve, spine, guts, id, ego, balls, and then eventually the good old libido and then what are you? A blob of useless Jell-o. An amoeba, a bed bug, a cockroach!"

"Aw come on, Arlene."

"You've got to work out this passivity before your inner drives turn against you and you become recyclable and I have to put you out once a week so that your still useful parts can go to help humanity. Your skin, forget about it—it'll be infested with the passive putz virus."

"Very funny."

"It's not funny. Look what will happen to you. You'll have huge medical problems just after you stumble through your fucking predictable and oh-so-boring midlife crises— prostate, heart, hypertension, even God forbid cancer, psoriasis, hemorrhoids—these are the common passive putz ailments. Then maybe you'll abjectly surrender to it all realizing something that you ought to have known all along which is that after all the turmoil, all the suffering and angst that you put us through you're probably not going to run away with that cute little shiksa you've been either dreaming of *shtupping* or even, in fact, have been *shtupping*."

"Oh please . . ."

"You're not going to go off and live in the woods like Thoreau . . ."

"The woods? I'd get Lyme disease."

"Or sail the seven seas or not even one sea."

"I get seasick just looking at a boat."

"You'll be a total wreck then you'll resign yourself to sticking your broken-down carcass, your worn-out psyche, and your barely alive libido with me, who by this time, you've made into a dishrag of a woman who will then have to fucking take care of you."

"Sickness and in health—remember?"

"How could I forget? Then it'll be a new car that's an almost sports car, bright sport jackets to hide the paunch, designer glasses, sporadic workouts, double up on crunches— but the spare tire doesn't deflate so you'll skip it and have another margarita and worry about working out next week. So in the end you stay married to 'the old ball and chain'— that's me, goddammit. You'll rationalize your fear and call it mature, reasonable, and sane. In truth you're just chicken shit. And then of course I mustn't leave out the expensive hooker at your annual convention, right?"

"I would never pay for it."

"I was hoping you'd say you'd never cheat on me."

"Oh, yes, that of course. Could I have my drink now?"

"You have to ask me?"

"You put me in an untenable position. If I don't drink it I'm showing you that I don't need a drink to bolster my courage. If I do drink it then I'm trying to bolster my courage and/or I'm showing you that I'm not a passive putz. Either way I lose."

"Okay, so what are you going to do?"

"If I'm a passive putz, what does that make you?"

"That's a good question."

"Do you want to marry a man like your father, the quintessential passive putz, if you will, though a totally nice guy."

"Don't call my father a passive putz—that's not respectful. He's a nice, loving dishrag, no, that's not nice either—he's easygoing, how's that, Pop? You're too easygoing, Pop. Yeah, I know, when he shrugs and gives into my mother . . . 'what can I do?' At that moment I could almost hate him but I love him. I don't always respect him because my mother pushes him around unmercifully but I love him because he loves me and even my rattlesnake sister—to love her you have to have more love in your heart than a thousand Jesuses. You're right.

I have to be honest with myself. A side of me really wants
a passive putz but not really. Jonathan, you have good stuff
in you. You don't have to be that way. You don't have to be
afraid of me, or any woman for that matter. You have to dig
inside of yourself. You can do it, Jonathan. You really can."

Jonathan puts the drink to his mouth and then puts it
down on the bar without drinking it.

Jonathan has made up his mind to try and see Beverly
again. If she'll see him he'll make sure to masturbate at least
one hour before they meet so that he'll be in control. He
hasn't made up his mind which woman he'll imagine he's
making love to yet. If it's Beverly herself then there's a danger
that his libido might get tired of her so that instead of being
too excited to contain himself he might be too jaded to get
excited. So he's been scouting around. The magazines don't do
it for him anymore and frankly the sexiest woman he knows
is his own ball-breaking fiancée who, unlike any other Jewish
woman he's ever even heard of, wants to fuck almost every
night. But if he masturbates on his own fiancée before he
sees Beverly he might become too guilty when he sees Beverly. When he sees Beverly, his mind has to be totally clear
of Arlene.

But now that whole thing with Timothy comes back to
him. The needy hungry little boy. Relationship. Mensch. Look
what he's about to do to poor Arlene. Planning not only to
fuck another woman but letting himself really fall in love
with her. Why not? Two kids not his own . . . an interracial
thing . . . a dangerous ex-husband. Fuck all that!

A real mensch can deal with that. Why settle for less than
your goddamn soul mate in life!?

He looks at the untouched drink in front of him. He
doesn't need the fucking thing. He turns to Arlene. He faces
her squarely.

"I'm not sure I'm ready to get married yet."

"Oh?"

"Yeah, not ready."

"Go on."

"Just not ready."

"Um-huh."

"Yet."

"Um-huh."

"Arlene, stop holding your glass that way."

Arlene has picked up her glass and she's holding it a few inches from his head as if she's going to brain him with it.

"I'm sorry, dear. I didn't mean to appear threatening."

Arlene apologizing for anything is like a snake coiling. Jonathan carefully takes the glass from her hand and puts it down on the bar.

"Any reason?" she asks calmly. Her calmness is worrying Jonathan. They have a date, a deposit on the hall; they've booked the rabbi—a Reformed woman rabbi with a lovely voice who will sing the ceremony. They booked a skiing honeymoon in Idaho. Their families have met and, as predicted, their mothers couldn't stand each other. Her younger sister is now pressuring her boyfriend to get married and her older married sister can't wait to get pregnant. Their fathers bonded and traded ailments.

Arlene is strangely calm. She agrees. They'll postpone.

Chapter Sixteen

The door to Jonathan's office opens and Beverly walks in. She moves into the client seat, sits, crosses her legs, looks directly at Jonathan, and hands him a referral slip.

Beverly Ovington Thornton, age 31, recently separated, suffering from anxiety.

They stare at each other awhile.

"I can't treat you," he states flatly.

"Why not?"

"I just can't. Let me refer you to someone else."

"No. I want you."

She stares him down. She seems implacable.

"Look . . ." he begins.

"You look," she interrupts. "I looked up that ethics thing on the American Psychological Association's website. We did not have a sexual relationship, which is forbidden until two years have passed since our therapeutic relationship ended so you can and you will treat me and it will be ethical. Totally ethical! Do you understand!?"

What happened to this demure, little (not so little really) seductress? Jonathan thinks. I don't want to treat her I want to . . .

He prevents himself from going further with that thought. Now after the shock of seeing her is wearing off he is able to look at her more objectively. He remembers how she looked when he first saw her, when she and her husband, that terrible Thaddeus Carmichael, came into his office for marriage counseling. She was carefully made-up, attractively dressed, oozing a kind of demure sexuality that instantly took possession of his all-too-vulnerable libido. Now she wears plain slacks, an oversized sweater, and very little makeup so that a guy can neither see her legs or her bust plus her formerly bedroom eyes have become steely. She is staring at him in a severe no-nonsense way that brooks no interference with her goal. All this gives him a creeping awareness that he does not have the inner resources or just plain willpower to say no and therefore leads him to reluctantly acknowledge that he might well be a passive putz after all.

"Look, I remember what you said to me when we met on Jamaica Avenue just a few days ago," Jonathan says.

"What did I say?"

"You don't remember?"

"Of course I remember. Do you?"

"'Jonathan, take me to a hotel,'" he says. "'I want to have one time with you—just one so I can remember it the rest of my life. I know we can't be together—I know there are too many obstacles . . . but that doesn't mean we can't . . . each of us have one beautiful memory in our lives.'"

She beams, "You remember."

"Of course I do. Every word. How could I forget?"

A tear comes to her eyes.

"Listen," he says as reasonably as he can, "I think that I'm in love with you. I think I fell in love with you from the moment I saw you." She tries to interrupt. "No, listen first.

Right now I'd like nothing more than to lock that door and take you on that couch and make love to you. So there's no way that I can be objective enough to treat you."

"You said you fell in love with me from the moment you saw me," she says.

"Well, something like that . . ."

"But look how you helped me even though you were in love with me. You made me face the fact that I was too motivated by material things. You have no idea how much that has helped me. My mother is like that and she helped instill that kind of thing in me. If you did not make me realize this problem, this shallowness, I would have gone on like that and I would have affected my daughter with these superficial values. All this you did for me while you were in love with me. Oh, Jonathan, don't you see?"

"Beverly, I can't treat you now and look at you at the same time."

"Then don't look at me."

"How can I . . . ?"

Beverly stands up, moves over to the couch, sits down, adjusts the pillow at one end of the couch, and suddenly lies down.

"What are you doing?" Jonathan asks, but he's beginning to know.

"This is what your Sigmund Freud used to do, right?"

"What do you mean by my Sigmund Freud?"

"Well, he was the first Jewish psychiatrist, wasn't he?"

"That sounds anti-Semitic."

"I am not a bigot. I was just pointing out the similarities between him and you."

"I have not been trained in the Freudian method."

"I think it's a great method," she argues. "My face cannot distract you while I can say whatever comes to my mind without suffering the embarrassment of looking at you straight in the eye. I've read all about it, you know. Now pull up your chair right behind my head and let's get started."

Craig is now a mess. Just as he had turned gay when he was a teenager, could he have suddenly turned straight at age twenty-eight? He'd never even heard of such a thing. All right then maybe he's turning bisexual.

But he doesn't want to be bisexual. He's quite happy being gay.

Now he becomes afraid to see Corcoran. There's a rehearsal this afternoon and they're supposed to go out for a couple of drinks with the guys and then they're supposed to go back to the new place and inaugurate it. Yesterday Corcoran whispered during a break in rehearsals that he couldn't wait to fool around in his brand new bedroom. Craig remembered being excited by the idea.

Godammit he couldn't have been excited yesterday if he was no longer gay today!

But that's because he loves Arlene. As a person, not as a woman! Yet he could not get by with telling himself that. He recalls the image of her lying on his couch completely nude. Her body so curvaceous, her face so sensual, just waiting for him to . . . and her breasts—omigod those mind-blowing breasts!

Ahhh he screams, he's getting a fucking hard-on just picturing them.

Maybe he should have done it. Why did he stop? What was he afraid of? Guys who've done it with women—bisexual guys and guys who'd been married or living with women—have described it in different ways. Some guys have said it was great, really much better than what gay guys do. Most if not all the guys he knows have, at one time, done it with a woman. All except him. When he found out who and what he was as a teenager it was gay all the way, at least until Arlene came into the picture. She's so funny and ballsy. Hey, maybe that's it. She's ballsy like a guy. But no she's ballsy like a woman. He loves her personality. Actually he loves her.

And she loves him too.

What the hell is he going to do?!

He's got to talk to Arlene.

"You were wrong," Jonathan tells Timothy the next time he sees him—not in a bar but in a diner over ham and eggs.

"Wrong? About what?" Timothy replies.

"You said the best way to get over a fantasy is to fuck it."

Timothy is sober now. He's drying out and wants to start living a constructive life. His last conversation with Jonathan about relationships and being a mensch really hit home with him. He's going to resume his practice as a sober, holistic therapist amongst the Indian tribes in Upstate New York. No, he's not pursuing Suzy who is now shacked up with a redneck and living in Colorado where they can get all the legal pot they want.

Jonathan will surely miss him but he realizes that he really needs a more conventional shrink.

"The best way to get over a fantasy is not to fuck it," Jonathan reiterates.

"Okay, so what is the best way?"

"To psychoanalyze it."

"Go on."

"She's making me shrink her. It's fucking mind numbing. I hear all about her childhood in Jamaica. Her overbearing father, her sneaky brother, and her rat-faced sister. Then on and on about her mother who is duplicitous, hypocritical, and of course hungry to hook up with a Jewish guy. She finds out that her mother was having an affair with some guy named Schine, a Jewish guy who owns a furniture store in Jamaica. But then instead of being shocked she's envious. She feels that Jewish guys hold the key to the magic kingdom which is located somewhere in Great Neck on the North Shore."

"I know where Great Neck is."

"She's lying there on the couch going on and fucking on. She comes with no makeup, baggy slacks, and an oversized sweater."

"Do you have any feelings, or should I say urges, as you see her lying there in front of you."

"I do."

"Go on."

"I want to run away."

"Oh?"

"I suffer from extreme ennui, torturous boredom, great relief when the time is up and then extreme trepidation when she's due again."

"But I thought you were really in love with her."

"You know a guy falls in love with a pretty face, a beautiful body, a sweet smile, lovely eyes . . . the whole nine yards but there's one thing he does not fall in love with . . ."

"What's that?"

"A tortured psyche, a confused, basically screwed-up personality disorder. When a beautiful woman lays all that bare, she strips herself of all the mystery behind her beauty."

"So?"

"So I want to get rid of her. Twice a week she comes in, lies on my couch and she doesn't stop talking for fifty minutes. I can't stand it anymore!"

Craig is unloading all his confusion on Arlene. He can't get it up with a guy anymore. Corcoran is fed up with his futile attempts to have sex and even more fed up with Craig's constant kvetching about it. So Arlene gets stark naked, throws herself down on Craig's beautiful new canopied bed, and gives him her best come-hither look. Craig gets out of his clothes, jumps into bed, kisses her fervently. But he can't get it up! He's flaccid, limp, slack, lifeless. He huffs, he puffs. She performs everything a woman can do, but as they say in Yiddish *gornisht helfen.* So then he suddenly moves off the bed. He's on the floor naked. He's shivering, crying, sweating, and mumbling gibberish. She covers him with a blanket. Arlene calls 911 and when the ambulance arrives she instructs them to go to Payne Whitney. She rides with him and checks him in.

Craig has had a nervous breakdown.

Jonathan is going to visit the same bar in SoHo where they once became engaged. Arlene tells herself the hell with him if he's not there this Friday night she'll start to make calls canceling the hall and the rabbi. She'll tell them to hold the deposit for now. She's got her eye on a guy in her office—he's not as cute as Jonathan but what the hell, age thirty is coming up soon.

So Arlene and Jonathan, their fantasies shattered, contrive to meet accidentally on purpose at the same SoHo bar where they became officially engaged. They drink, kiss, hug, go back to Arlene's apartment, get high, make love, and renew their wedding plans. Jonathan insists that the now sober Timothy be invited to their wedding and Arlene, impressed by her fiancé's new resolve, gives in immediately. She is enthralled by Jonathan's assertive behavior.

And so they marry and live *kvetchingly* ever after.